Half Moon Ranch – Rodeo Rocky

Half Moon Ranch – Rodeo Rocky

by Jenny Oldfield

Half Moon Ranch – Rodeo Rocky
Copyright: © 1999 Jenny Oldfield
First published in Great Britain in 1999 by Hodder Children's Books

The right of Jenny Oldfield to be identified as the
Author of this Work has been asserted by her in accordance
with the Copyright, Designs and Patents Act 1988.

Original title: Half Moon Ranch 2 – Rodeo Rocky
Cover and inside illustrations copyright: © 1999 Paul Hunt
Cover layout: Stabenfeldt A/S
Typeset by Roberta L. Melzl
Editor: Bobbie Chase
Printed in Germany, 2006

ISBN: 1-933343-40-0

Stabenfeldt, Inc.
457 North Main Street
Danbury, CT 06811
www.pony.us

1

"Yup, I guess over the years I broke just about every bone in my body," Hadley Crane told Kirstie Scott.

The head wrangler at Half-Moon Ranch leaned on the fence at San Luis Competition Grounds to reminisce. His white Stetson was pulled well forward to shield his lined, brown face; his gray eyes were alert to the activity in the arena.

Kirstie too watched the team-roping competition with mounting interest. The next steer was made ready, prodded and pushed into the narrow wooden chute. Two riders entered chutes to either side. They sat astride tough, well-built quarter horses – horses that had been trained to round up cattle on the ranches that nestled in the foothills of the Colorado Rockies. The nerves of both riders and horses were strung tight as the steer barged and kicked inside its narrow trap, demanding to be released into the arena.

"I broke my left leg three times," Hadley went on. "My hip got trampled, I dislocated this right shoulder more times than I can count . . ."

"All in rodeo accidents?" Kirstie stood on the bottom bar of the white fence to get a better view. The barrier went up, the steer charged into the dusty ring.

"Sure thing; mostly bulldogging. That's a mighty risky event, when you have to land on eight hundred pounds of steer and wrestle him down. And bronco riding; that's bad too." Hadley watched the red steer raise the dust as it skidded to a halt across the arena, turned right around and charged back the way it had come.

After a ten second delay, the two cowboys were let loose too. Whooping and yelling, digging their spurs deep into the horses' flanks and with the cries of a sizeable San Luis crowd in their ears, they swung their ropes and headed for the steer.

Kirstie winced as the first rope circled the steer's head and the noose tightened. The frightened animal was dragged to a sudden halt. Now it kicked and writhed as the second cowboy swung his lasso. She glanced up and read the bold words printed on the banner that fluttered in the breeze over the entrance to the arena: "Keeping the Dream Alive!"

"I always feel sorry for the steers," she told Hadley quietly.

The ex-rodeo man shrugged and smiled briefly. "Yup. But I reckon you're soft on any critter with four legs. Seems to me, you like 'em better than the two-legged kind."

Kirstie didn't deny it. She watched the second cowboy, the heeler, lasso the steer's back legs and jerk him to the ground. The poor animal lay bound and helpless in the dust as the horses pranced and the riders dismounted.

"Nine point six seconds!" the voice on the loudspeaker announced. The crowd of two thousand people roared and cheered.

Quickly they untied the defeated animal and cleared the arena, ready for the next team. Scores flashed up on the electric scoreboard.

"Hey, Kirstie." Lisa Goodman sidled up to her friend to watch the closing stages of the competition. She wrinkled her nose at the gray dust that blew out of the arena, then brushed her white sweatshirt and ran a hand through her curly red hair.

"Hey," Kirstie replied, eyes narrowed and fixed on the next steer lined up in the chute.

"Remind me never to wear white to the rodeo," Lisa grumbled, squinting down at her grubby sweatshirt.

"Never wear white . . ." Kirstie began.

Lisa jostled her sideways. "Not now – next time!"

"*What* next time?" As Kirstie turned to glance at her best friend, the wind blew her blonde hair in wisps across her hot face. There was grit in her eyes and a growing sensation that this would be her last visit to the competition grounds. "Tell me never to come to another rodeo again," she countered.

"OK, never come . . ." Lisa's voice was drowned by the cheers of the crowd as the final steer was released.

"Isn't this great?"

"Wow, did you see that last team? Nine point two seconds to rope that steer!"

"It came out of the squeeze like a black bullet! Those guys sure knew how to rope a steer!"

Eager voices commented on the team-roping event as the crowd waited for the result

"OK, Kirstie?" Sandy Scott joined her daughter, Lisa and Hadley at the ringside. A taller, older version of Kirstie, with the same blonde hair and large, gray eyes, she wore a pale straw Stetson and light denim shirt over her blue jeans and tan cowboy boots, and was followed by a bunch of guests from Half-Moon Ranch.

"Hmm." Kirstie chewed her lip and said nothing, knowing that the rodeo wasn't her mom's favorite thing either. It was the ranch guests whose eyes had lit up when they heard about the regular San Luis event. They'd asked Sandy to drive them the fifteen miles into town, so they could cheer, clap, take photographs and enjoy the hustle and bustle of the July show day.

"What's next?" one hyped-up kid asked Hadley. The dark-haired, eleven-year-old boy climbed up on the fence and sat kicking his heels against the wooden rails. He looked eagerly across the arena toward the empty chutes.

"Wild horse race," the wrangler mumbled, low and slow. "You have teams of three men trying to get a saddle on a wild mustang and ride him around that track, see?" He pointed toward a racecourse that ran for half a mile around the perimeter of the competition grounds. "Course, the mustang don't wanna know. He was out on the plains of Wyoming a couple of days back, before they drove a truck out there to rope him in and drive him here specially for the competition."

"Cool!" Brett, the young kid, was impressed.

"After that it's the bulldogging event, and last of all comes the bronc riding," Sandy told him. "Then back home to Half-Moon Ranch for a cookout by Five Mile Creek."

Brett Lavin nodded and switched his gum from cheek to cheek. His father, Dale, told him to stay put while he went to place a bet on his favored team for the wild horse race.

Amidst the excited chatter and the people milling about, Kirstie kept her eyes on the empty corral beyond the arena. "What happens to the mustangs after the race?" she asked Hadley in a quiet voice. It was a question she'd never considered in the four years she'd been living at the ranch.

"They end up down at the sale barn," the wrangler explained, as he nodded to a couple of old friends, tall, skinny men in checked shirts and Stetsons like Hadley himself. "If they're lucky, a rancher like Jim Mullins at Lazy B, or Wes Logan up at Ponderosa Pines will pay good money for them, break them in and use them as working horses on the cattle round-ups in spring and fall."

"And if they're not lucky?" Lisa cut in.

Hadley shrugged. "Some of these ex-rodeo horses are real mean. There's not a lot you can do with 'em."

As Kirstie weighed up his answer and the uncomfortable silence that followed, she frowned. "They wouldn't be mean if they were allowed to stay out in Wyoming where they belong. No horse is *born* mean!"

Brett Lavin had latched onto what he sensed might be an argument between the old ranch hand and the boss's daughter. He clicked his gum between his teeth and stared intently.

Sandy caught Kirstie's eye and gave a small shake of her head. "Not now!" she whispered.

"Hey, why don't we go over to the corral to watch them unload the horses from the truck?" Lisa suggested brightly, linking arms with Kirstie and dragging her away.

"Am I right?" Kirstie insisted as the two girls threaded their way through the crowd. "Do you know any horse that's born mean?"

"OK, OK, don't yell at me!" Lisa cut through a group of cowboys who stood waiting for the results of the team-roping event. When the scoreboard flashed up the winners to another loud cheer, the men turned to shake hands. "I'm on your side, remember."

Though she had lived all her life in the small town, and

her mother, Bonnie Goodman, ran the End of Trail Diner on San Luis's main street, Lisa spent a lot of her time at her grandfather's place in the mountains.

It was there, at Lone Elm Trailer Park, that Kirstie had first met and made friends with the red-haired girl during the Scotts' first summer at Half-Moon Ranch. They'd been nine years old and had swapped friendship bracelets at the end of the school vacation, before Kirstie had started her first semester at San Luis Middle School.

Since then, at exactly the same point in the year, when the aspen trees were silver-green in the mountain valleys and the clear lakes sparkled under deep blue skies, the girls had ridden out to Hummingbird Rock and exchanged new bracelets. Four bracelets for four years of friendship.

"Sorry," Kirstie told Lisa now, as they arrived at the corral where a large truck was backing in. Two men ran to the rear of the truck to lower a ramp, and before the girls had time to take in what was happening, a bunch of horses clattered down the metal slope.

Noise, sudden light, strange smells. The mustangs emerged from the trucks with nostrils flared and ears set back. They wore rough rope headcollars and trailed lead ropes after them. There were grays and blacks, tan horses and sorrels, Appaloosas and paints, all with long, flowing manes and frightened eyes. They kicked and bucked as they came out of the truck, rearing up in the bright sunlight, their hooves flailing and thudding into the dust.

Holding her breath, half in horror at the conditions in

which the horses had been kept, half fascinated by their wild strength and beauty, Kirstie stared.

Soon a second truck backed into the corral to deliver more horses for the race. The ramp went down with a clatter and the mustangs fled from their dark prison. They squealed and whinnied, heads thrown back, eyes rolling in fear. And this time, Kirstie fixed her gaze on one particular horse.

He was a beautiful bay stallion with a jet-black mane and tail; bigger than the rest and first out of the silver truck. And he was crazy. He bucked and kicked, twisted, spun around on the spot, head down, thumping the ground. The sun shone on his rich brown coat; his strong shoulders and rump rippled with muscle as he screamed out his protest at being torn away from his endless plains, his sea of grass, his wilderness, to be dumped here, inside this circle of wooden barriers and curious, staring faces.

"Say!" A spectator whistled and sighed at the sight of the magnificent horse. "That's where I'd put my money if I was a betting man!"

"A real rodeo champion," his neighbor agreed.

The horse reared and threw back his head just feet from where Kirstie and Lisa stood.

Kirstie couldn't take her eyes off the bay horse. She heard the men's amused talk, and wondered how they could treat it so lightly. She gasped as a wrangler darted toward the horse, seized the fifteen-foot lead rope and began to drag him across the corral. The horse fought back, pulling his head away and almost wrenching the rope out of the man's hands. But he was hemmed in by other mustangs, all led by wranglers who crowded them toward the wooden chutes that led into the main arena. He was forced to go with the flow.

Then he was in a chute, a barrier came down behind him, and he was trapped once more.

"Look at him kick!" The man next to Kirstie had followed the progress of the big bay horse.

"Rodeo Rocky!" his friend added, chuckling at the wild horse's antics inside the squeeze. He gave him a name that seemed to suit his bucking, kicking tricks. "Yeah, I'll put five dollars on that horse. Five on Rodeo Rocky; make no mistake!"

The starting-pistol had fired and the wild horse race had begun.

Kirstie's attention was glued on Rodeo Rocky as he bucked and kicked his way into the arena. She ignored the teams of men standing with saddles inside the ring, the fresh cheers, and the announcements over the loudspeaker. She had eyes only for the bay.

Between her and Rocky was a fence. Men with numbers on their backs were running to catch hold of trailing lead ropes as other horses charged and twisted, skidded and spun. Dust was rising; there was a terrible heat and a feeling of fear.

"Rocky was a lead-horse," she whispered to Lisa through gritted teeth. "You can tell he was in charge of the herd by the way he handles himself."

13

The stallion stood his ground amidst the chaos. His ears were flat, his eyes were hard. Kirstie saw him curl back his lip and snake his neck to bite the cowboy who approached him. The man leaped back just in time.

"Grab the rope, Jake!" he yelled to one of his partners.

A thickset wrangler in black T-shirt and jeans managed to take hold of the end of Rocky's lead rope and twist it around his waist. He dug in his heels and leaned back with all his weight as the horse reared and pulled.

"Jake Mooney's the anchor man in black," Sandy Scott told the girls. "He's the best there is."

Kirstie hadn't heard her mother approach as the race began, but she didn't turn around. Instead, she nodded and kept her gaze fixed on Rodeo Rocky.

"He's got Gary Robbins on his team as mugger." Kirstie's mom put one foot up on the bottom rail of the fence and leaned forward.

The mugger was the man whose job was to take hold of the taut rope and ease his way along toward the struggling horse. Kirstie knew what would happen next; Robbins would soon grasp the horse around the neck in a headlock, and then reach out and pinch the top lip hard. The horse would squeal with pain and, while the hurt was bad, the third team member would dart in with the saddle. Before the horse knew what was happening, the cinch would be buckled under his belly, and the rider would be on his back.

"Gee, d'you see that?" a spectator cried.

Kirstie gasped and gripped hold of the fence.

Rocky had twisted his head free of the mugger's lock and strained against the anchor man. By now, other teams had saddled and mounted their horses. Robbins swore and moved in to try again.

This time he grappled and succeeded in squeezing the bay horse's lip. Almost buckling at the knees from the pain, the stallion didn't resist as the saddle was slapped over his back. Kirstie closed her eyes for a second, and then forced them open. Now the rider, Fenney Brooks, was up in the saddle, the mugger had released his grip and the anchor man flung the lead rope into Fenney's outstretched hands.

"He's off!" the bystander yelled. "Man, see that bay horse go!"

Man and rider were almost last out of the arena onto the track, but they were catching up fast. Fenney was digging in his spurs; the horse's stride was long. They ate up the ground between them and the leading horses.

"This is awful!" Kirstie groaned at the sight of the rider's spurs. She left her spot by the fence and ran along the front of the crowded stand to the spot where the horses would thunder across the finish line. She heard Lisa coming after her. "Did you see that?" she cried.

Hundreds of yards away, across the far side of the dirt track, the wild horses bunched together around the bend. The riders steered with the lead rope, wrenching their horses' heads to the left and right, spurring them on. One rider on the outside of the bunch lost his balance and crashed to the ground, curling up to protect his head from the thudding hooves. The crowd oohed and aahed. Then a brown horse went down, kicking up dirt as he went, falling onto his knees and rolling sideways.

"I know; I can't look either!" Lisa hissed. Like Kirstie, she'd hidden her face behind her hands. "Was it Rocky?"

Kirstie shook her head and squeezed forward for a view of the finish. She jumped up and down, dodged heads, and slipped to the front of the crowd. "Here they come!" she breathed, almost choking at the sight of the horses thundering toward them. "Rocky's leading . . . He's gonna win . . . Yes, yes, he is!"

Horses and riders flashed by in a blur of faded color behind a cloud of thick dust. Kirstie glimpsed bay and black, silver spurs cutting into flanks, the saddle leather, the raised arm, the whip . . .

There was a deafening cheer, more shouting and spurring as the slower horses finished the race. Riders slid from the saddle, muggers and anchormen ran to join them. Mooney and Robbins slapped Fenney Brooks on the back as he stood by his sweating, bleeding horse.

Slowly Kirstie released her pent-up breath. She fought back the sob that rose high in her throat as she stared at the trickles of blood from the cuts in Rodeo Rocky's heaving flanks. Then she glanced up at the fluttering banner above his head as Brooks took the lead rope and dragged him back into the arena to receive first prize.

The bay stallion pulled away. His head was high, his jaw rigid, his back arched. He stood below the white banner that flapped in the cold wind blowing off the Meltwater Mountains.

"Keeping the Dream Alive!" Kirstie re-read the bold red letters.

She gazed again at the wild horse that had been torn from his world, trapped, tied and ridden to exhaustion. And, as she glimpsed the nightmare in his eyes, she swore to him that she would help.

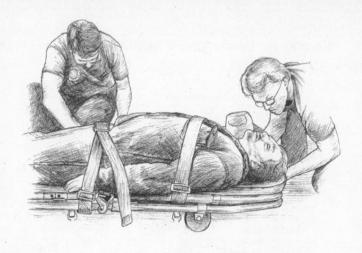

2

"One rider broke his jaw." Hadley's report on the wild horse race was in full swing when Kirstie, her mom and Lisa rejoined the group from Half-Moon Ranch. Dale Lavin was smiling broadly and showing the other guests his winnings, while his son crowed in a loud voice over the way the cowboys had used their spurs to urge the mustangs on.

"You see that Fenney Brooks?" he cried, running to meet Kirstie and Lisa. "I wanna ride like him, without a bridle. You see him? You see how he beat those other guys?"

Kirstie frowned and nodded. "You wanna break your jaw too?" she muttered under her breath.

"Kirstie!" Sandy Scott stood between her and the guests. "Why don't you and Lisa just find a good place to watch the bulldogging and the bronc riding? Meet us back here at four thirty."

Kirstie hung her head and scuffed the dirt with the toe of her boot. "Do we have to? Can't we leave before the end of the show?"

"Not unless you want to walk the fifteen miles home," Sandy said firmly, grabbing her by the shoulders and turning her away.

"I don't want to see it," Kirstie complained. "I can't stomach much more, Mom."

Seeing that Kirstie was serious, her mother kept one arm around her shoulder and walked her a little way off from the group. "What's gotten under your skin, honey?"

The poor bay stallion, she wanted to say. *The cuts from the spurs; the look in his eyes.* But she was too choked to speak.

"Rodeo Rocky," Lisa said quietly, coming up alongside Sandy and Kirstie and sticking out her chin in a determined fashion. "We say that's no way to treat a beautiful horse!"

"I agree," Sandy replied. "But what can we do? You saw how the crowd loved it. And the rodeos have been treating horses pretty rough for years and years. Are we gonna be the only ones to speak out?"

Kirstie took a deep breath and looked her mom in the eye. "Yeah. Someone has to."

"Then we'd be *real* popular with the ranchers and the rodeo organizers!" Sandy shook her head.

"So?" In Kirstie's mind, unpopularity was a price worth paying.

"So, we'd lose business," her mother pointed out. "Which we can't afford to do. We rely on people hearing good things about Half-Moon Ranch, to make them want to come and stay."

"Your mom's right," Lisa said after a pause.

Kirstie glared at her, as if to say, whose side are you on?

"Sorry." Lisa shrugged helplessly and wandered off to watch the bulldogging event just getting under way in the main arena. There was a buzz in the crowd again, as the first riders galloped into the ring to either side of an angry steer.

Kirstie was left face to face with Sandy. "Don't spoil the day," her mother warned. "I know it's hard, honey, but try and put a good face on . . . for my sake, OK?"

Out of the corner of her eye, Kirstie saw the bulldogger leap from his horse and wrap his arms around the thick neck of the bucking steer. Within seconds, the man had grabbed the bull's horns, twisted his head and flipped him sideways into the dust. "OK," she agreed. "But I don't have to watch this. I'll be over by the corral if you want me."

"Fine." Her mom watched her go with a sigh, and then went back to her guests.

At least if I wait by the corral I can watch the horses being saddled for the bronc event, Kirstie thought. Being with horses, anywhere, any time, was her main thing.

20

But today, even the pleasure of watching her favorite animal was spoiled by knowing that the wranglers were forcing saddles on their backs and dragging them into chutes. She felt a dull anger come over her as she made her way toward the corral and the scores for the bulldogging event went up on the board. Ignoring the cheers and the yells, she found a quiet corner where she could sit on the fence and wait out the rest of the afternoon.

Half an hour passed in a haze of dusty heat. The cheers of the crowd sounded distant to Kirstie, whose gaze was fixed on the broncs in the corral. The unbroken horses milled restlessly in the confined space. One would break from the group and make a quick, nervy run toward the fence, spin and lope back. Another would raise his head and rear as a wrangler approached to cut him out of the herd. The cowboy would swing his lasso, the horse would feel the rope snake around his neck and burn into his skin as the man dug his heels in the dirt and pulled.

One horse, a flea-bitten gray, gave her wrangler a hard time before she was finally forced into the squeeze. Too strong for one man, she jerked the cowboy off his feet and dragged him through the dust. Kirstie heard the man yell, saw two others race to help. They lassoed the gray mare's hind leg, and then hobbled her by winding the rope around her neck, pulling the back leg forward off the ground. Then they dragged her, limping off-balance, into a chute.

"Gary, that flea-bitten's your bronc!" a nasal voice yelled across the corral. The middle-aged speaker was a man Kirstie recognized with a shiver of dislike. It was Wade Williams, the owner and organizer of the San Luis Rodeo. He was tall and broad, with a sallow face and a heavy, dark moustache. "You got that?" he shouted at Gary Robbins, one of the riders in the bronc event.

The cowboy strode around the outside of the corral, hat in hand, leather chaps flapping against his legs.

"You're first into the arena!" Williams instructed. "Then Fenney on horse number 9!"

Kirstie sighed as the cowboys prepared for action. She saw Jake Mooney, the anchor man from the team-roping contest, speak with the organizer, who jerked his thumb toward the horse Mooney would be riding. She glanced in the direction of Williams's pointing finger, then stood up and clung onto the fence in dismay.

This couldn't be right. The stallion earmarked for the heavyweight cowboy was Rodeo Rocky!

Kirstie looked again to make sure. The bay horse trotted defiantly around the edge of the corral, his black tail swinging, the blood on his flanks now dry and congealed in long, dirty streaks. He wove in and out of the other horses, twisting and turning whenever a wrangler drew near.

"He's a tough one," Wade Williams warned Jake Mooney.

"Yup." Jake remembered the lead stallion all too well from the wild horse race.

"Think you can ride the buck out of him?"

"Sure," came the careless reply.

As the men discussed Mooney's chances, Kirstie stepped down from the fence and drew nearer to the chutes. How could they think of putting Rocky through even more than he'd already undergone? Wasn't one cruel race enough?

It was because Rocky had shown such spirit in the first event, she decided. Williams must see him as a big crowd pleaser, a real challenge even for the likes of Jake Mooney. With her heart sinking, her mouth feeling dry and her palms beginning to sweat, she watched the wranglers set to work on getting the bay horse into a squeeze.

And now events really did begin to blur and slide. As the lasso snaked around Rocky's neck and he reared up with an angry cry, the bulldogging contest came to an end and the first bronc rider was released into the arena. There was a wild cry from the crowd, a few seconds of tension as Gary Robbins kept astride the bucking, kicking gray.

"No!" Kirstie whispered, staring at the badly-cut bay stallion. A second wrangler moved in on Rocky to hobble him. The horse fought the lassos for all he was worth.

"Come away, honey," a quiet voice at her shoulder said. "If you can't stomach it, come and sit in the car."

She turned to her mother. "Mom, look what they're doing to Rocky. Make them stop!"

"I can't, Kirstie." Sandy Scott took hold of her daughter's hand.

Over her shoulder, Kirstie saw Gary Robbins hanging onto the reins of his gray mare for dear life. One arm flung wide, head down, leaning back in the saddle, he rode the bucking bronc around the arena.

She turned back from the competition to the corral. "Look! Now they're using an electric prod to force Rocky into the chute!"

Sandy grimaced. The metal prods were used on the ranches to maneuver cattle into the branding pens. As the electrified rod touched the bay's sore flanks, he whinnied and leaped sideways, into the path of a second wrangler, ready to pull the hobble rope tight.

At that second, a gasp and groan from the crowd told Kirstie and Sandy that Gary Robbins' bronc had finally succeeded in unseating her rider. There was a lull while the cowboy's time was recorded and he picked himself up from the dust. Now it was Fenney Brooks's turn on Number 9, a black and white paint.

Meanwhile, Rocky was prodded and forced into the chute closest to where the Scotts stood. The wranglers slammed the gate shut behind him, and one ran for the heavy saddle to make him ready for his turn in the competition.

Next, Kirstie saw Fenney shoot out of squeeze number 2 on the frightened paint. The slim, supple rider rode the horse's frantic bucks with ease at first, dipping and swaying, maintaining a perfect balance. Soon it would be Rocky and Mooney's turn. She groaned and half-closed her eyes as the wranglers slammed the saddle across his back and leaned through the gaps in the chute fence to fasten the cinch strap across the gashes in the horse's sides. How

24

long now before Mooney jumped into the saddle and the chute opened?

But there was a delay. The crowd had stopped cheering. There were gasps and cries. A cloud of dust rose from the arena, and when it cleared, Kirstie could see Fenney Brooks down on the ground. He lay flat on his back without moving. The black and white horse, suddenly free of his rider, reared up over the lifeless body and thudded his hooves down within inches of the man's head.

Kirstie gasped too and ran toward the arena. In the eerie silence following the fall, she saw the wind catch Brooks's hat and roll it toward the fence. Then men were climbing the fence and running. One caught hold of the horse's reins to drag him clear. Another knelt over the rider, called for a stretcher and brought more helpers scrambling into the ring.

"It's crazy!" Kirstie whispered to Sandy, who hovered behind her. "Mom, can't you see, this is all completely crazy?"

Without waiting for an answer, Kirstie ducked between the bars of the fence and ran into the arena. She saw Fenney Brooks stir and try to lift his head as a stretcher arrived. In the confusion, she was able to make it to the far side and grab hold of Wade Williams by the arm. "You gotta stop them!" she yelled above the anxious swell of noise amongst the spectators.

Busy directing the rescue operation, the rodeo organizer tried to pull his arm free. When Kirstie hung on, he glanced around at her, his face red and angry, the corners of his mouth turned down beneath the heavy black moustache.

25

"They've used an electric prod on the bay stallion!" she cried. "He's already cut from the earlier race. No way is this fair!"

The tall man frowned and pushed her to one side. Kirstie lost her balance and had to put out a hand to stop herself from falling into the dirt. Then she was up and following him across the arena to the squeezes.

Williams stopped short of Rocky's chute and turned on her. "Quit it, will you?" With a quick look sideways, he gestured to Jake Mooney to get ready to mount his horse, which kicked and barged inside the trap. "Soon as they've carried Fenney clear and got him into an ambulance, you're on!" he yelled.

The tough cowboy nodded and pulled on his black leather gloves. As he climbed the chute fence, poised ready to swing his leg across the protesting horse, his silver spurs clinked and glinted.

"Please!" Kirstie cried. She ran around to face the angry organizer. "You have to stop this!"

"I said, quit it! Do you have any idea what you're asking?" His voice nasty and loaded with scorn, Williams stood by Rocky's chute and stared down at her.

Kirstie held his gaze. She clenched her hands until her nails dug into the soft palms. "Use another horse!" she pleaded. "Rocky's hurt. Don't send him into the ring!"

The organizer sneered and shook his head. "Come here, let me tell you something." He leaned into the chute and roughly took hold of the bay stallion's reins.

Squinting into the sun, Kirstie saw Rocky pull away, eyes rolling, ears back. Above them, balanced on the top rung of the fence, Jake Mooney's black figure towered.

"What you gotta understand, little girl, is that this bronc is special," Williams explained. "He's strong, he's fast and he's mean. If we play our cards right, we'll make a champ out of him!"

"What kind of champion?" Kirstie protested. She was stung by the organizer's insulting tone, but felt hot, dizzy and helpless before him.

Rocky strained away from the man's grasp, swinging his head, shaking his tangled mane.

"A prize bronc. We'll send him around the circuit; San Luis, Renegade, Marlowe County."

Inside the narrow chute, Rocky reared and whinnied.

Williams held onto the reins, dragging the horse down. "Then, in the fall, when he's got himself a big name as a bucking bronc, we'll truck him up to the Denver sale barn and sell him for thousands of dollars."

Kirstie swallowed hard and bit her lip. She saw her mom quickly push her way to the front of the crowd, climb the fence and jump into the arena.

No way! She cried to herself, gazing up with tear-filled eyes at the struggling horse. *No way will we let that happen*!

3

"I'll give you two thousand dollars for the horse." Sandy Scott's offer came across quiet and firm. Her hand shaded her eyes from the sun's rays, which caught her blonde hair and made it shine the color of corn.

Taken aback, Wade Williams let go of Rocky's rein. "You can't be serious!"

"I've never been more serious in my life." Kirstie's mom didn't waver. She stood beside the chute, one hand on the back pocket that held her checkbook.

Kirstie felt she could hardly breathe. She really loved

her mom, she decided. She loved her more than anything in the world!

"Two thousand dollars," Sandy repeated. "But only if you sell me the stallion *before* you let Jake ride him."

"Hey, boss!" The cowboy climbed down from the fence to protest. "You can't do that. I'm down to ride the bay. It's a big chance for me."

The frown on Williams' face deepened. He batted his hand in Mooney's direction, as if swatting a fly. "Let's get this straight. You want to buy Rodeo Rocky here and take him to work at Half-Moon Ranch?"

"You got it," Sandy replied. She glanced sideways at Kirstie and gave a brief smile.

"Hmm." The rodeo organizer turned over the offer in his mind, while in the center of the arena a team of paramedics worked smoothly to get the injured Fenney Brooks safely strapped onto the stretcher. The quiet crowd watched intently for signs that one of their favorite riders was going to make it through the accident.

"Well?" Kirstie's mother pushed for a reply.

"This is a great horse we're talking about." Wade's tone had changed. The sneers had gone and he turned on the smooth talk. "He has a good head and eye, and a mighty fine, deep chest."

"Sure," Sandy agreed. "And two thousand is a good offer. You can take it or leave it."

Kirstie squeezed her eyes shut. *Please, please, please say yes.*

29

"I reckon I could get twenty five hundred in the fall," Williams said. A shrewd tone crept into his high, nasal voice and his eyes narrowed.

"Sure thing!" Jake Mooney encouraged.

"Maybe, maybe not." Sandy Scott was on a level with Williams when it came to making a deal. "Sure you could if the horse does well on the summer circuit. But if he doesn't, you won't get more than a thousand for him in Denver. Whereas, if you do business with me, you take the nice fat check home with you tonight."

"Hmm." Wade grunted and pulled nervously at his moustache. He glanced quickly at the saddled bronc, and then along the line at other horses trapped in chutes, awaiting their turn in the ring. "Take horse number 12," he snapped at Jake without looking at him, and reaching out a hand to shake with Sandy over the deal.

Yes! Kirstie raised her clenched fists in front of her. Then she ran to the bay stallion and leaped onto the fence. "We bought you!" she cried. "Mom paid a fortune. You belong to us!"

The check written, the show went on without Rodeo Rocky.

"I sure as heck hope this check don't bounce!" Wade Williams sneered at Sandy as he pocketed the check.

"It won't." Kirstie's mother was already looking around for help to take the stallion out of the chute and get him fixed up for transport back to the ranch. Lisa had watched the sale of the horse from the edge of the arena and had volunteered to run and find her grandpa to see if he could oblige.

"D'you know what you've taken on here?" Williams couldn't resist talking down to Sandy. "It don't take a lot of savvy to figure out that you've just bought yourself a whole bunch of trouble."

"But you just said yourself that Rocky was a great horse!" Kirstie protested. In the background, she could hear the yells start up as, in place of Rocky, Jake rode a pure white horse into the arena.

"Sure, a great *rodeo* horse." Williams stepped aside to let Kirstie and Sandy get a full view of their bargain. Inside the chute, Rocky still kicked and battered himself against the bars of his cage. "Meaning wild and mean."

"Only because he hated it in the truck!" Kirstie claimed. "And because he's been tied up and prodded and forced to do what he doesn't want to do!"

"Yeah, sure." Satisfied with the deal, the organizer shrugged. "Come back and tell me that in a couple of weeks, after you've tried to break him." He turned his back and strolled off, leaving them to back their horse out of the squeeze and deal with him as best they could.

"Don't listen to him!" Kirstie told Sandy.

Hadley was nowhere to be seen, and they were still waiting for Lisa to show up with Lennie Goodman and a solution to the ride home with Rodeo Rocky. Meanwhile, two of the wranglers had stepped in to help them back the

31

wild horse into the empty corral. After a few difficult minutes, they'd succeeded in getting close enough to open the back gate of the chute and let him find his own way out. Rocky had backed up, kicking and writhing, then lashed out with his heels when he found himself free of the trap. He'd run himself to a standstill around the corral and stood now, breathing heavily, covered in flecks of sweat, at the other side of the corral.

"We've got our work cut out for us," Sandy murmured, looking him over with a practiced eye.

"But we'll do it!" Still brimming over with joy that they'd saved the stallion from the rodeo, Kirstie wouldn't let doubts cloud her day. She looked around eagerly for Lisa.

"It'll mean tightening our belts for the rest of the summer," her mother warned. "We paid more than we could afford. Maybe we'll even have to sell one or two horses in the Half-Moon remuda to make up some of the money."

Kirstie only half-heard. She'd spotted Lisa and her grandpa pushing through the crowd to join them.

"Still, we made the decision," Sandy said more firmly. "And I'm glad. Rocky's a fine horse!"

"A *great* horse!" A smile spread across Kirstie's face as she spoke the words. A beautiful, free-spirited wild stallion with the wide open plains of Wyoming in his blood and a dream of liberty in his head.

* * *

"That's sure good of you, Lennie." Sandy Scott gladly accept-ed the trailer park owner's offer of a lift home for Half-Moon Ranch's new horse.

"Lucky I drove down with the horse trailer," the old man told her, keeping a wary eye on Rocky as he backed the pickup truck through the gate of the corral. "I brought it for a friend to do some business at the sale barn tomorrow, but I sure don't mind helping you folks out." He leaned out of the driver's window and jerked his gray head toward the mustang. "I hear you paid out a lot of money for this guy?"

As Sandy, Lisa and Kirstie got to work unbolting the trailer ramp, Sandy explained how the surprise deal had come about. "We plan to work with the horse for a few weeks, get him used to the others in the remuda, put a saddle on his back and gradually train him to be part of the trail-riding team."

"But first you got to get him home." Lennie jumped from the cab and took a good look at Rocky, who had raised his head and tensed up at the sight and sound of the truck and trailer. Lisa's small, wiry grandfather kept his distance while he decided how they were going to persuade the horse into the box. "Are you gonna leave that saddle on him?" he asked.

"We don't have a choice," Kirstie told him. "We can't get close enough to take it off."

"No problem. Hadley or Charlie can bring it down to Wade tomorrow." Sandy rolled back her sleeves and began to move quietly toward the horse. "Easy, boy," she murmured, stopping to wait a while as Rocky pawed the ground, and then reared up. His lead rope swung loose, the end knocking against his legs as he landed.

As they waited for the horse to settle down, Kirstie spotted Hadley standing quietly by the gate. He'd been showing the Half-Moon guests around the rodeo grounds, but now she stole over and drew him to one side to give him the good news. "Look what we bought for the ranch!"

"Yeah, I heard." The old ranch hand scarcely opened his mouth to reply. He studied the stallion with narrowed eyes. "Reminds me of a saying my first ranch boss used to have way back," he muttered. "Old Wes Douglas. His number one rule was, 'A horse is a dangerous machine. You hurt him first, or he'll hurt you.'"

"Oh, no way!" Kirstie shot back. The idea of inflicting more pain on Rodeo Rocky went against everything she felt and believed.

"You got some other way of showing him who's boss?"

She flicked her hair back from her face. "Maybe."

Before an argument with the old wrangler could develop, Kirstie went to help her mother. Sandy had edged in toward the bay stallion and reached forward, slow and smooth, to grasp the end of the lead rope, which trailed along the ground. She stood up without tightening it. "Good boy!" she said.

Rocky's eyes rolled as he breathed in Sandy's smell. He backed off into a corner, pulling the rope taut as he went. The second he realized she was holding it, he jerked his strong neck and whipped it from her hand.

"OK, I could do with some help," Sandy called, giving up the patient approach. Soon the corral would be needed again, so they would have to work faster to get Rocky out.

Hadley and Lennie moved up alongside her and Kirstie, keeping the horse pinned against the fence. Though Kirstie didn't like it, she had to stand by as Hadley beckoned a couple of rodeo workers to join them with lassos at the ready. Almost before she knew it, the ropes were thrown around Rocky's head and the struggle began again.

The stallion kicked and strained. He skittered and twisted, reared up, then trampled the dusty ground.

"Bring the truck up close!" Hadley yelled at Lennie, who ran to reverse the trailer.

"Stand clear!" Sandy warned the girls.

The men took the strain on the ropes as Rocky bucked and reared, the low rumble of the truck's engine sending him into another frenzy of defiance.

"Move him forward!" Hadley grunted.

"Yes, sir!" One of the rodeo men whipped the end of a rope down hard on the horse's buttock. The sudden pain shot Rocky forwards toward the lowered ramp. His hooves clattered against it as once more the man whipped him on.

Kirstie swallowed hard, longing for the episode to be done with. Soon, soon they would be able to set Rocky loose in Red Fox Meadow, by the cool, clear water of Five Mile Creek.

But meanwhile, he would have to endure the dark, stuffy trailer, the slam of the door as the ramp went up, the rocking and swaying of the journey home. Inside the metal box, the horse stamped and screamed.

"OK, Let's go!" Sandy said quickly. "Kirstie and Lisa, you ride with Lennie. Hadley and I will follow with the ranch guests."

As they sprang into action and Lisa ran around the front of the trailer to jump in her grandfather's cab, Kirstie paused long enough to see a look pass between her mom and Hadley. She overheard a snatch of quiet conversation before Lisa yelled for her to join them in the cab.

"Don't look at me like that!" Sandy protested. "I know what I'm doing."

"What did I say?" Hadley shrugged as he slotted the last bolts of the raised ramp into place.

"You don't have to say anything. It's the way you look."

The skeptical old ranch hand shrugged again.

"So, go ahead, say it!" Sandy challenged. "Say what's on your mind."

Hadley stood up straight, listening to the horse throwing himself around inside the trailer. "OK," he nodded, with a glance at Kirstie as she climbed into the cab. He spoke under his breath, so that she had to strain to hear. "You want to know something? I think you just made a big – I mean a BIG – mistake!"

* * *

The round pen by the barn was empty except for Jitterbug

and Lucky when Lennie Goodman pulled in through the arched entrance of Half-Moon Ranch. The other horses were out in the meadow, enjoying a well-earned afternoon's rest.

Kirstie's older brother, Matt, looked up from the work he was doing with the palomino and the sorrel. He quickly unhitched the lunge rein from Jitterbug's halter, looped it over the white fence and strode across the yard to greet the truck as it parked by the gate of the pen.

"What the . . .?" Hearing the disturbance from inside the trailer, Matt stopped short.

"We'll tell you later!" Kirstie thrust open the door and jumped down. It had been fifteen miles of torture for Rocky on the twisting, rough road out of town along Route 5, almost an hour of torment for Kirstie and Lisa as they tried to block their ears to the horse's frightened squeals. Now they had to unload him from Lennie's trailer and get him into the safety of the fenced pen.

Too busy to answer Matt's puzzled questions, she left her brother to Lennie Goodman and urged Lisa to help her lower the ramp.

"No, wait!" Lisa looked around the empty yard and across at the barn. She yelled at a figure standing in the wide doorway. "Charlie! We could do with some help!"

The young, dark-haired ranch hand threw down a rake and came running. When he reached the trailer and peered inside, he gave a low whistle. "Wow!"

"Let's get him out!" Kirstie pulled at the heavy bolts, anxious to free Rocky from his ordeal. "Open the gate, Charlie."

Charlie Miller swung into action without asking any questions. He set the open gate to form a barrier that would stop the stallion from running off across the yard, then he ran around to the far side of the trailer to join Lennie and Matt, who were by now ready for the horse to come out. Once they were in place, Kirstie slid the last bolt free and lowered the ramp.

Rocky reacted to the sudden light and rush of fresh air into the trailer by ducking his head and charging. Out he came, clattering over the metal onto firm ground, past the three men and two girls, who stepped back to avoid his flying hooves. He sensed the sky above, the snow-capped mountains in the distance, the river water running through the valley. Freedom.

He was out of the trailer into the round pen, going wild, his rodeo saddle wrenched to one side, stirrups swinging wide, dirt flying from under his feet.

"Wow!" Charlie breathed. "Some horse!"

"Watch out!" Matt yelled at Kirstie and Lisa, as Rocky raced around the edge of the pen, too close for comfort.

Driven crazy by forty-eight nightmare hours, the wild stallion careered toward Kirstie's own horse, Lucky, and the skittish sorrel that Matt had been working with when they arrived.

Jitterbug saw Rocky charge at her. Head high, dancing nervously in his path, she seemed not to know which way to turn.

"Get out of the way!" Once more Matt yelled a warning and waved his arms above his head.

Lucky took heed and trotted quickly to the far side of the pen. But the dainty mare froze as Rocky charged. The stallion bared his teeth, snatched at her neck and missed. He wheeled around, kicking savagely, striking out at the horse that stood in his way. The kicks landed with a thud. Jitterbug squealed and sank to her knees.

Seconds later, when Rocky had charged on and the dust had cleared, Kirstie saw the mare splayed out. Blood trickled from her nose. A dark red stain seeped slowly into the pale yellow ground.

4

The sun was low and red-gold over Eagle's Peak when the vet, Glen Woodford, arrived from San Luis. Aspens and oaks rustled in the breeze on the banks of the creek, where a dozen ranch guests enjoyed the usual Thursday evening cookout of barbecued chicken.

The visitors had arrived back at Half-Moon with Hadley and Sandy only minutes after Rodeo Rocky had brought Jitterbug down with his savage kick. Shocked at first, they'd quickly gotten over the incident, and were now relaxing out-doors, listening to Dale Lavin play guitar as the sun went down.

"It's a good thing you called me out," Glen told Sandy Scott as he examined the sorrel mare's cut face.

Kirstie stood in the background, behind her mother and brother, beside a subdued Lisa.

"She bled real bad!" Lisa whispered with a small shudder.

"Sure." The vet cleaned the gash on the horse's nose with a white gauze pad. "There's an artery that runs right down this side, see. There's always a lot of bleeding when a blood vessel is damaged."

Kirstie recalled how Hadley and Charlie had held Rocky at bay while she and Lisa helped Jitterbug to her feet and out of the round pen into the nearby barn. She glanced down at her hands to see that they were streaked with dried blood from the sorrel's injury.

By the time Matt had run to the ranch house to call the vet, Sandy had driven through the ranch gates to be greeted by the chaotic scene. Just thirty minutes later, her mom had settled the guests and Glen had arrived.

"Who put pressure on the wound to stop the bleeding?" the vet asked, taking suture equipment out of his bag and injecting a local anesthetic before he stitched the gash.

"Kirstie did." Lisa gave her friend a worried smile. "She didn't freak out. She just went ahead and did first aid until her mom got here."

"That's good." Glen Woodford worked quickly and skillfully, kneeling in the straw beside the injured horse. His closely cropped, dark hair was flecked with gray, his tanned face marked with fine lines under the eyes. "It

41

means she stands a better chance of a quick recovery. We don't need to give her a transfusion; just a few sutures, a shot of antibiotics, a top-up of sedatives, and she'll be just fine."

"Poor Jitterbug." Sandy crouched down beside the vet. "I bet you never knew what hit you."

As Glen finished his work and clicked his bag shut, he looked around at the watching group. "So where's the brute who did this?"

"Still in the round pen," Matt reported, his face lined with a deep frown. "I cleared Lucky out of there real quick, but the bay made it plain he wasn't going anywhere."

"So let's take a look at him." The vet led the way out of the barn and into the lengthening shadows of the corral. The round pen stood beyond the area where the horses were saddled and made ready for the daily trail rides, behind the long, low wooden tack room.

"I don't think the bay was hurt," Matt said in a cold, unsympathetic voice. "He's just too crazy to know what he was doing."

Kirstie followed silently, unable to argue for Rocky. But she understood why he'd done it. "I'd like to see how they'd all act if they'd been treated the way he was!" she muttered to Lisa.

"I guess." The uneasy answer came as the two girls arrived at the pen.

The bay stallion stood in the deep shadow cast by the tack room wall. His coat looked almost black, and the whites of his eyes glinted eerily as he stamped his feet and tossed his head.

Glen Woodford leaned against the fence and took a long hard look. "That's a fine, big horse," was his first comment.

"But?" Matt prompted, guessing from the vet's tone that there was more to follow.

"But he's a horse with problems, that's for sure. See how he pushes his nose in the air, walks backwards, plays up every which way he can?"

They all observed Rocky's restless antics.

"What are you saying?" Matt's voice broke the silence.

"I'm saying, first you have to keep this horse away from the others," Glen told them firmly. "The mean streak that made him kick Jitterbug could run deep. And second, you can try working with him the way you would with other mustangs; roping him and getting him used to bit and bridle. But don't go getting your hopes up too high."

"Meaning?" Kirstie's brother gave her a meaningful look, making sure she got the message.

Glen Woodford sighed and took a long time to answer. He'd turned from the pen and begun to walk toward his Jeep, parked by the ranch house, before he delivered his final verdict on the stallion. "You can try, as I said. You put in all the work; spend hours, days, weeks with the lunge rein here in the round pen, but my guess is you still won't break this horse!"

"The point is, we don't want to *break* him!" Kirstie insisted.

Deep down she felt that the vet had been wrong about Rodeo Rocky.

The Scott family sat around the kitchen table with Hadley and Charlie. Lennie and Lisa had left them arguing over the day's events and driven onto Lone Elm. Now the door onto the porch stood open to let in the cool evening air. Kirstie watched the tiny hummingbirds hover around the birdfeeder in the dim dusk light, seeing them dart their long beaks into the honeyed water in the dish.

"So tell me how you plan to work with the horse if you don't want to break him?" Matt pushed aside his empty plate and leaned his elbows on the table. "No, don't tell me. I don't have six hours to listen right now."

Kirstie screwed her face into a frown. There was no point arguing with her brother in this mood. She looked to her mother for support, but Sandy Scott sat silent and worried.

"You paid two thousand dollars for a horse no one can ride!" Matt repeated a sentence he'd muttered several times during supper.

Across the table, Hadley caught his eye and shrugged.

"Give him a couple of days," Charlie Miller broke in quietly. They were the first words he'd spoken, either during or after the meal, and he came across shy and awkward as usual. Until January of that year, Charlie had been a college student with Matt in Denver. But he'd grown sick of the city and the rat race and decided to take time out by working as a wrangler on the Scotts' dude ranch. He'd learned the job quickly under Hadley's guidance, showing skill at handling the hard-working quarter horses and mustangs, and leading the trail rides with quiet confidence.

"It'll take more than a couple of days," Matt objected, reminding them of Glen Woodford's verdict on the problem horse.

Sandy sighed and scraped back her chair as she stood up. "This isn't getting us anywhere. On the one hand, Glen knows what he's talking about better than most. And you too, Hadley. I respect your judgment."

Kirstie's heart sank as she listened to her mom. If the experts were against Rocky, what future did he have here at Half-Moon Ranch?

"On the other hand, I did make a decision back there. OK, so it was a spur of the moment thing, but I reckon I know a good horse. And you have to agree, this is a great looking animal!"

Kirstie sat up and nodded. She found she was holding her breath as the family conference moved on.

"Maybe we should give him a chance," Sandy said slowly, gazing out at the hovering, darting birds.

"Or maybe we should cut our losses and send him to the sale barn right now." Matt didn't mean to be harsh, but he made it clear that he and Hadley were the only ones talking sense. "If not, we put the other horses at risk, just like Jitterbug today."

"And the guests," Hadley put in. "You put a dude on that bay stallion, he bucks him off, the guy breaks a leg. Then you kiss your good name goodbye."

45

"Good point," Matt agreed. "Honestly, Mom, it'd be crazy to even try!"

"Hmm." Sandy went to lean against the doorframe and gaze out across the corral at Red Fox Meadow beyond.

Kirstie followed her. "A couple of days for him to settle down, Mom," she said quietly. "Please."

A new moon had appeared over Bear Hunt Overlook; a pale silver circle in a fading blue sky. Across the yard, in the round pen by the tack room, the shadowy figure of Rodeo Rocky could be seen standing absolutely still, ears pricked, listening to the sounds of the mountains.

Sandy glanced down at Kirstie's earnest face. She lifted a hand to smooth her windblown hair. "OK," she said softly. "A couple of days. Let's see how it goes."

"I don't know a whole lot of technical stuff about horses," Charlie admitted when he met up with Kirstie in the round pen early next morning. "Compared with Hadley, I'm a rookie."

"I don't care. I'm just glad you want to help." Feeling sure that she and Charlie were on the same wavelength, Kirstie zipped her red fleece jacket up to her chin and tucked her hair inside the collar. At the far side of the pen, Rodeo Rocky kept his wary distance.

"I reckon you have to stay back and just watch a horse before you try to get to know him," the young wrangler went on. "Give him a chance to decide you're OK, and no way are you gonna hurt him."

46

"Me too." She grinned at Charlie. "See Rocky watching us now. Most people would move right in before he's ready, and start putting a rope around his neck and lunging him. I don't like that. Not until he's happy about it."

Charlie grunted and nodded in Rocky's direction. "Look at him lift his tail and high step around the pen!"

The stallion had decided to take a look at his two visitors. Instead of keeping the furthest distance from them, he began to trot in a circle that went around behind their backs about five yards from where they stood. As he trotted, he kept one ear pointed forward, but his inside ear was flicked toward Kirstie and Charlie.

"At least he's OK about us being in the pen with him." Kirstie let Rocky trot around and around, head up, ear constantly flicking in their direction. "That's one step up on last night." She recalled the screams of anger and fright as they'd unloaded Rocky from the trailer, the way he'd lashed out at poor, unsuspecting Jitterbug.

The first rays of the sun caught the horse's dark bay flanks, giving his coat a coppery sheen.

"What do you reckon, fifteen hands high?" Charlie asked quietly, happy for Rocky to tighten his circle and trot closer in to where they stood.

"Maybe more." Kirstie didn't feel a grain of fear as the stallion moved in. She thought it was wonderful the way his coat shone with the metallic gleam. It made him special, let him stand out from other normal bays. And the black mane and tail gave a contrast. Once they were combed through

47

and the coat was brushed and groomed, Rocky would be the finest looking horse at the ranch. "It's amazing!" she sighed. "Twenty-four hours ago, this horse was going through the worst time of his life. Locked up, tied up, shoved and prodded. You'd think it'd make him hate the sight of us."

But no. As they stood quiet in the long, cool dawn shadows, Rocky was dipping his head and tightening his circle. *What's this?* He was asking them. *What do you want?*

He came closer, slowing to a walk, still moving in a cautious circle but ready to talk.

Then, across the neighboring corral, the tack room door opened and Hadley stepped out with a heavy saddle. The door flapped and banged against the wall as the old wrangler called out to them. "Charlie, time to fetch the horses in from the meadow!"

As if reacting to an electrical current, the sudden noise made Rocky veer away from his patient observers. He swung out to the edge of the pen, loping at high speed in wide, reckless circles.

Charlie sighed and shrugged. "Sorry."

"That's OK." Kirstie knew he was paid to take orders from Hadley. At least they'd had a few quiet minutes of making friends with Rocky. She smiled at Charlie as he fixed his pale straw Stetson firmly onto his forehead and went to do his first job of the day.

And things are better than yesterday, she decided. She left the round pen as smoothly and silently as she could.

Meanwhile, Rocky loped on, pushed by his instinct to flee at the first sign of danger.

Once through the gate, Kirstie turned to watch him run. Yesterday, Rocky had fought anything that went near him. Today he'd let her and Charlie stand in the pen. Yesterday, he'd been full of hate. Today he was curious, questioning, thoughtful.

It was a small step forward. But it was a step all the same.

"How's it going?" Sandy asked as she crossed paths with Kirstie on her way out to the corral.

"Good!" Her head was up, shoulders back as she went into the ranch house for a quick breakfast of blueberry muffins and juice.

5

"How's the rodeo horse?" Brett Lavin asked Kirstie over lunch, his mouth full of hamburger and fries.

"Good!"

"How's it going with the bucking bronc?"

"Has he kicked any more horses in the face yet?"

The questions had come thick and fast as ranch guests came out of their cabins, crisscrossed the yard and rode out on the trails.

Kirstie had spent the morning on the ranch instead of taking Lucky out with one of the trail groups. Her plan was to hang around in the yard and the corral, where Rocky would be able to see her come and go. He would learn to recognize her from a distance, watch her at work, see her riding quietly by on her palomino as she took him to drink at the creek. With the guests out trekking toward Miners' Ridge or Elk Rock, the place was peaceful, with nothing to disturb the lone stallion in his round pen.

"So how's it going?" Sandy Scott wanted to know after lunch. She'd just come out of the barn where she'd checked on Jitterbug's cut nose, and was rushing to head up the afternoon ride through Fat Man's Squeeze to Deer Lake. But she stopped for a moment outside the tack room to get a real answer about the problem horse out of her non-committal daughter. "Come on, Kirstie, give me the lowdown!"

"Better than yesterday." Out of the corner of her eye, she noticed Rocky standing by the fence, looking out at the bunch of horses saddled and waiting in the corral. The clink of bridles and squeak of leather as riders mounted had caught his attention, and he stood alert and puzzled.

"Have you tried him on a lunge rope?" Sandy asked.

"Not yet. He needs more time."

Her mom mounted Johnny Mohawk, a pretty, high-spirited, half-Arabian horse whose black coat shone in the full force of the afternoon sun. She swung her leg easily over the saddle and sat looking down quizzically at Kirstie. "How much time?"

"Couple of days."

"Sunday? Then, no doubt a couple more days after that. And before you know it, the horse has been living in the pen a whole week. You realize we need the space for Yukon's foal as soon as she gives birth." Sandy reminded her that their six-year-old brown and white mare was in the late stage of pregnancy, and that both mother and baby would take priority in the pen.

"That's OK. Rocky will be ready to move into Red Fox Meadow by then," Kirstie assured her, not letting her mom see that this was a pressure she could do without. Behind her cheerful front, Kirstie couldn't yet see a realistic prospect of letting the wild mustang loose.

And as Sandy rode the guests off to the lake under the bluest of blue skies, Kirstie chose a firmer approach for the afternoon. She would go into the round pen, she decided, but not with a halter and a lunge rope. They would remind Rocky too much of yesterday's rodeo. There would just be herself and the horse.

"Good luck!" Charlie passed by on Moose, a big, gray quarter horse, as Kirstie swung open the gate into the round pen. He gave a long look over his shoulder, and then loped on to catch up with Sandy's group.

The gate clicked behind her and she stood, as relaxed as she could manage, waiting for Rocky to get used to her entrance into his private ring.

The horse gave her his full attention. His tail swished from side to side, and he stamped the ground once.

Kirstie took a couple of steps toward him, and then

stopped. She looked up at Eagle's Peak and across at the ranch house; anywhere but in Rocky's direction. But she could judge where he was by sounds. He'd begun to trot. Around the rim of the pen he came, one ear straight ahead, one ear flicked toward her. He snorted and ducked his head, and kept on trotting.

Still Kirstie pretended she wasn't paying attention. She wandered a few steps to her right, then to her left, and turned around on the spot, waiting for the moment when curiosity would get the better of the horse.

And sure enough, his circle grew tighter, as it had before breakfast that morning. It was Rocky's way of asking a question; What do you want?

Nothing. She let him know her answer by turning her head away. *No pressure.*

So, come on, what do you want? He slowed down, came closer.

Kirstie could feel the heat from his body, his warm breath on her bare arms. He was reading her body language the way she wanted, sensing that, far from being a threat to him, she was here to make friends.

And now he stopped and lowered his head, poking his nose toward her as she stood in the center of the pen. He nudged her arm. *Come on, you must have some reason for being here.*

Kirstie felt a thrill of excitement. Here was this crazy, untamable horse coming up to her and giving her a friendly shove; the savage horse that only yesterday had kicked and bucked and bitten. Keeping a wide smile on her face, murmuring soft words of encouragement, she reached out her hand to stroke him.

*   *   *

"Wow!" It was Saturday morning, and Lisa had dropped in at Half-Moon Ranch with her mother, Bonnie. She was leaning on the fence, watching Kirstie work with Rodeo Rocky.

Less than two days in, and Kirstie felt she was well on the way to winning the horse's trust. True, he would still sometimes shy away when she walked into the pen. His ears would flatten and he would quickly put the biggest possible distance between them. But mostly he would allow her into the pen, take his time, and then wander toward her, head lowered, licking his lips in friendly greeting.

"How do you do that without a lead rope?" Lisa wanted to know as she watched Kirstie rub Rocky's face and shoulders.

"I don't know. It kind of happens, I guess." She'd followed her gut feeling that the horse must not be forced. When he was good and ready, he would come up and talk.

She proved it now by running her fingers down his strong, supple neck and listening to him snort with pleasure. Still she took care not to stare directly at him, knowing that, like all horses, Rocky would take this as a threat. And she'd learned how to move when he was around; slow and smooth, sideways and in circles, never fast and direct.

"How long did it take?" Lisa was obviously impressed. She gestured for Matt to get up from the porch swing where he was reading a book and come and look.

"A lot of hours. And we're not completely there yet. He *thinks* he can trust me, but he still has to be sure!" Kirstie showed her friend how she could sometimes drop her hands to her side, walk a few steps away and have Rocky follow her of his own accord.

"What do you think?" Lisa turned excitedly to Kirstie's brother.

"So far, so good," he conceded, ready to wander back to his book.

"Isn't Kirstie cool?" Grabbing his shirt sleeve, Lisa insisted that he stay to watch. She shone a bright smile at dark-haired, good-looking Matt. "Can you believe she did that so quickly?"

Matt shrugged. "Yeah, yeah. But you wait till she tries to put a bit in his mouth and a saddle on his back."

"Party pooper!" Lisa made a face and turned back to Kirstie, who was letting Rocky nuzzle softly at the palm of her hand. The horse was blowing and nibbling, nipping at the hem of her T-shirt, following everywhere she went. "Take no notice of Matt!" Lisa called. "It's a guy thing!"

"What's a guy thing?" Kirstie walked slowly toward her friend with Rocky in tow.

Lisa grinned and leaned over the fence to say hello to the stallion. "Matt knows he was wrong about this horse," she explained. "And guys don't like that. They like to be right!"

Sunday afternoon. Sandy Scott had dropped the old guests off at the Denver airport and was driving back to Half-Moon Ranch with a bunch of new visitors for the start of a fresh week of trail rides, cookouts, sing-alongs and quiet evening walks by the side of Five Mile Creek.

Kirstie had stayed behind to work with Rocky because Yukon was expected to foal tonight and that would mean taking the stallion out of the round pen and letting the new mother look after her foal in safety. Yet Kirstie mustn't let Rocky feel that they were under pressure. The horse had to be willing to leave the pen and join the others in the meadow.

"Get Hadley or Charlie if Yukon shows any signs of going into labor," Sandy had instructed before she left for the airport, knowing that Kirstie would be the one closest to the barn where the pregnant mare was stabled.

But so far, all was quiet. Matt was in San Luis visiting his girlfriend, Lachelle Jordan. Hadley was holed up in his bunkhouse, enjoying the few slack moments that his job allowed, and Charlie was the only one around to watch Kirstie's afternoon session with the rodeo horse.

"I'm gonna try him with a halter and lead rope," she decided after half an hour of the friendly stuff that Rocky by now so obviously enjoyed. The horse was happy to let her stroke and pat him from head to toe and had no thought of fleeing or acting up in his handsome head. "We have to get a rope on him to lead him out to the pasture when he has to leave the pen."

Charlie nodded and went into the tack room. Moments

later, he emerged with the rope and harness and quietly handed them over the fence to Kirstie.

"This is your first big test," she told the horse softly, letting the rope and collar hang unnoticed, as she hoped, from her right hand.

But Rocky had spotted the equipment. He tensed up and backed off, then craned his head to sniff at the rope.

"Trust me, it doesn't mean we're gonna tie you up and beat you like Wade Williams' men," she promised, swinging the collar toward him to let him get a proper sight of it now. "It's what we do around here to get a horse from point A to point B. No pain involved, no problem."

Charlie grinned. "I sure hope he can understand what you're saying!"

Kirstie smiled back. "Every word! Can't you, Rocky?" She offered him the halter to smell and explore. Then after a while she made her move, doing her best to look more confident than she felt. "Now this slips on over your nose, like so."

The horse blinked as the harness slid over his face. *Easy, easy; please don't fight it*! And that was it. The buckle was fastened, nice and easy. For the first time since he arrived at the ranch, Rocky was wearing a headcollar.

That night, when the new moon was high, Sandy Scott called Kirstie from her bed to come and watch Yukon's foal being born.

"Any moment now," she promised as they crossed the

yard and entered the barn. They passed by a row of empty stalls until they came to a well-lit, straw-lined one at the end. The stall was fourteen feet square, allowing plenty of room for the brown and white broodmare, while her helpers, Charlie and Hadley, stood outside at the ready.

"How do we know it's about to happen?" Kirstie whispered from outside the stall. The birth of a foal was a rare event on the ranch, since Sandy usually bought three-year-olds from the sale barn, ready to be trained and ridden.

"Yukon's been restless all day," her mom explained. "She's been lying down, getting up, biting her flanks and so on. Then, about an hour ago, her contractions started."

Rubbing her eyes, which were still prickly from sleep, Kirstie stared.

"This is it," Hadley murmured. His expert eye had caught sight of the foal presenting itself in the birth canal. He showed Kirstie a pair of small front feet, explained that the foal would be in a diving position. The feet should soon be followed by the nose, neck and shoulders.

"Don't we help or something?" she whispered.

"No, she's doing fine," her mother told her. "We only step in if there's a problem."

Already the foal was slithering onto the hay, safely delivered by the mare. Then it rolled and wriggled inside the birth sac, breaking through and beginning to breathe of its own accord. As it did this, Kirstie found that she let go of her own held breath. She gave a deep sigh of relief.

"Now, the foal will try to get to her feet." Hadley described the next stage. "The cord should break and we treat the end with iodine solution. See, she's having a shot at standing up right now!"

Kirstie nodded. The tiny, fragile creature with its enormous head was wobbling up on skinny legs. Kirstie gasped as the baby fell and lay still.

"Too soon," Sandy reported. "Give her a few minutes' rest and she'll try again."

Fascinated, Kirstie watched every movement of the newborn creature; the alert flick of her ears, the struggle to rise. Meanwhile, Yukon accepted her foal by licking her clean and nudging her onto her feet.

"When will she start feeding?" Charlie's eager question broke the soft, warm silence of the barn. It made Kirstie realize that this birth was the first the young wrangler had seen.

"In a couple of hours." Hadley's easy, calm reply showed that he'd witnessed it many times. "And come morning, both broodmare and foal should go out into the round pen for exercise." He turned questioningly to Sandy Scott.

Sandy nodded. "I know. I warned you all that we'd have to move Rocky."

For the first time since she'd crept out of her warm bed to watch the birth, a feeling of unease came over Kirstie. Sure, she'd known about the deadline, but she'd been pushing it to the back of her mind. She turned away nervously and pictured Rocky out there in his safe pen under the silver moon.

"That's OK," Charlie encouraged. "You can move him into the meadow, no problem."

"You think so?"

"Sure. He's wearing a headcollar. He'll let you fix the rope and lead him out."

Taking a deep breath, she nodded.

"Let Hadley do it," Sandy suggested, picking up Kirstie's nervousness.

"No, that's OK." Bad idea! There was only one person that Rocky had learned to trust. Kirstie knew it had to be her and no one else.

"Before breakfast," her mom insisted. Satisfied that all had gone well for Yukon and her foal, she led the way through the dark barn out into the yard. They walked in the moon and starlight, by the round pen.

For a moment, Kirstie paused to glance over the fence. There was Rocky, awake and alert to the sound of their footsteps, keeping his distance, listening, and looking. The copper gleam of his coat under the moon was weird, the black of his mane like a moving shadow, and the glint of his eye wary as his gaze followed their journey from barn to house.

"Tomorrow I'll take you to Red Fox Meadow," Kirstie murmured to him through the darkness. "It'll be fine, you wait and see!"

6

Rocky had to want to do it. Kirstie recognized the first rule about working with horses. If he wasn't willing to go into the meadow, nothing short of the extreme violence used by the wranglers at San Luis rodeo could make him.

"This is going to be OK," she told him gently, choosing the first light of Monday morning when the sun peeped over the hills behind the guest cabins to go out into the round pen. With everyone except Hadley and Charlie still fast asleep, she knew there would be no distractions.

But she still had to convince the horse that she herself

was calm and easy about the move. She had to enter the pen with halter and lead rope as if there was nothing unusual, nothing threatening about to happen. There must be a smile on her face, the same casual, indirect approach as ever. As she drew near and looked up at his intelligent, sensitive face, she stroked his neck and murmured encouraging words. "OK, you're doing great. I'm gonna slip this head-collar on and we're gonna walk right out of here into Red Fox Meadow."

Slowly, with the shadow of suspicion gradually melting from his eyes, Rocky let her ease the collar over his nose and strap it behind his ears. He dipped his head and nuzzled her arm.

"Let's walk." Giving the gentlest of tugs on the lead rope, she set off for the gate.

The big bay stallion followed quietly, his coat gleaming, his dark mane blowing in the breeze. He scarcely looked at the gate as they stepped outside the pen into the yard, his ears forward, then twitching this way and that.

"*Goo-ood* boy!" Kirstie headed for the wooden bridge across Five Mile Creek. Beyond that lay the meadow, where Hadley and Charlie were already cutting out from the herd the horses that would be needed for the day's rides. "This is gonna feel kind of strange," she told Rocky, as their footsteps echoed on the thick pine planks that formed the bridge. "You're gonna meet Cadillac and Crazy Horse out here. Cadillac's the big, creamy-white mustang and he knows he's beautiful, but don't let that bother you. Then there's Crazy Horse. Crazy Horse has to be the ugliest horse around, but he thinks he's a good-looking guy, just like Cadillac. You can't come between those two; they go everyplace together . . ."

As she chatted on about other horses in the pasture, Kirstie led Rodeo Rocky along the side of the creek toward the long stretch of high fence that formed one side of the field where they kept the Half-Moon horses at grass. The field began broad and flat, then sloped upwards, away from the creek, and narrowed so that the whole shape was a six-hundred foot long, sloping triangle laid out at the foot of Hummingbird Rock. At the far end, she spotted Charlie on Moose, working to cut Johnny Mohawk out of the herd and head him toward the ranch.

She paused with Rocky at the wide gate into the meadow, beside a big clump of tall blue irises. The mustang sniffed at the flowers, ignored them and craned his neck to reach golden marsh marigolds growing closer to the banks of the fast flowing creek. As he chomped on the juicy dark green leaves, Kirstie saw Lucky trot across the meadow to greet her. The palomino's pale mane and tail swung as he came, his head was up, and the sun shone on his golden coat.

Rocky turned at the sound of approaching hooves. For a moment, as his lip curled back and he bared his teeth, Kirstie feared a problem. Up till now, since he'd been kept alone in the round pen, she'd given Rocky her undivided attention. But Lucky was her special horse and no way was

63

she going to ignore him for Rocky's sake. She wondered if it was possible for a horse to be jealous; if her talking to the palomino and making a fuss over him would throw Rocky into a mean mood.

She decided to tether his lead rope to the fence-post just in case. He watched her carefully as she tied the slip-knot, then he eyed the palomino.

"Hey." Kirstie stood clear of the bay horse and leaned over to say hello to Lucky. She rubbed his neck, and then laid her cheek against his cheek. Then she stroked his nose and stepped back.

How had Rocky taken it, she wondered?

The bay stallion had his head up, his eye fixed on Lucky. He tugged at the rope, found he had nowhere to go and stamped his feet. Kirstie went back to him more warily than before. "This is Lucky," she told him, as the palomino approached them calmly from the other side of the fence. He was as tall and strong as the wild horse; a match if the two decided to fight.

Rocky flared his nostrils and whinnied loudly. He turned his head quizzically to Kirstie.

This is like being a new kid in school, she thought suddenly. *The new kid doesn't know anyone, feels awkward and left out. The teacher enlists a confident, friendly kid from the class to help the newcomer settle in*. The comparison made her smile and relax. She went back to Lucky. "Rocky's new here," she explained, half-laughing now. It was crazy to talk to a horse like this, and yet she knew somehow that both

Lucky and Rocky were getting the picture. "He needs some help. I'm gonna lead him into the field to join the group. You have to show him how, OK?"

Lucky leaned over the fence and snorted.

Quickly Kirstie went to untie Rocky's lead rope. "And we know you're a big, tough guy," she told him briskly. "But we don't want you throwing your weight around just to prove it." She led him firmly to the gate, opened it and took him into the field. The horse looked at the small herd of fifteen ranch horses in the distance, glanced sideways at Lucky and dipped his head.

It was the moment for Kirstie to unclip the lead rope. One smooth movement and Rocky was loose. She held her breath, watching every sign: the head, the ears, the eyes.

It was Lucky who made the first move. He came right on up to the powerful newcomer, wiggling his ears and blinking. For a split second Rocky held back, switching his tail, staring, telling him, 'Keep your distance.' But Lucky ignored the message. He thrust his nose toward the bay horse, his sensitive nostrils sniffing, then breathing out noisily. Then he walked right around the back of him, saying, "You could kick me if you had a mind to, but I don't think you're gonna do that."

Quietly Kirstie watched and smiled. Lucky came full circle, back to Rocky's face. He made a trot away, came back, danced a bit, trotted again.

"Go!" Kirstie urged the new horse.

He waited a few more seconds, trying to decide. Should he stay? Should he go? At last, he crouched back onto his haunches and launched himself across the meadow after Lucky. His hooves sank into the soft turf, his tail streamed behind him. Soon the two horses were thundering the length of Red Fox Meadow, matching each other stride for stride, as the rest of the herd stood quietly by.

"Neat!" Charlie said as he rode by with Johnny Mohawk, heading for the ranch.

Kirstie nodded with a satisfied grin. She slung the rope over her shoulder, shut the gate after Charlie and went to tell her mom: No problem, Rodeo Rocky was doing fine.

"Here's how I see it." Kirstie helped at the cookout by serving barbecued chicken to the guests and explaining her theory about Rodeo Rocky to anyone who would listen.

It was one week after the ex-rodeo horse had joined the Half-Moon remuda, and as far as Kirstie was concerned he'd been behaving like an angel. Now Sandy Scott, Lennie Goodman, Lisa and Matt were considering the transformation that had come over the big bay horse.

Kirstie spooned barbecue sauce over the plates, then waved the ladle around. "No horse is born mean. He only gets mean if someone treats him roughly. So, with Rocky, he had one bad experience and it scared him real bad. For two days he went crazy."

"Hey!" Lisa protested, as a splatter of barbecue sauce narrowly missed her clean blue T-shirt.

Kirstie ignored her friend. "*You'd be crazy* if you'd been kidnapped and forced into some dark truck that roared you away from the beautiful place you'd lived in all your life!"

"Sshh, honey!" Sandy took the sauce ladle from her and made her serve salads instead, hoping she could do less harm.

". . . So!" Kirstie didn't even notice that she'd changed jobs; she was so excited about Rocky's progress. "To Rocky, it seemed like all men are the enemy!"

"Sure." Matt conceded this much. "But you're saying you've worked with him and gotten rid of this crazy streak?" All week he'd remained doubtful, and it seemed he wasn't about to change his mind.

Kirstie nodded. "He's smart; very smart. It only takes him twenty-four hours in the round pen to know all men aren't the enemy after all. He checks me out and decides I'm OK, for a start. I'm talking to him, I'm feeding him, I'm taking him out to the meadow and showing him where to find the best grass."

"He knows you're with him, not against him!" Out of range of Kirstie's waving arms, Lisa gave her friend some warm support. "Have you been out to the meadow to see him with the other horses?" she asked Matt and Sandy. "The herd gives him respect because he's big and strong . . ."

". . . Except for Silver Flash," Kirstie put in. The big sorrel with the white blaze down her nose hadn't exactly given Rocky a warm welcome.

"OK, and poor Jitterbug wasn't too happy either," Lisa admitted. "But there's been no real trouble. Lucky made sure of that. He took to Rocky, showed him around really well."

"Lucky's been great," Kirstie agreed, drowning Lennie Goodman's salad in dressing. "He stuck with Rocky. Now it's Cadillac and Crazy Horse; Lucky and Rocky. No one can get between those two pairs any more!"

"Well, that's great." Kirstie's mom was genuinely pleased. "I've been checking Rocky out all week, and I agree with you, you wouldn't know him as the same horse as the one we drove up from San Luis."

"So when does he start earning back what we paid for him?" Matt stacked used plates on a nearby table. "Meaning, when do we put someone on his back and let him ride out on the trails?"

There was a pause. Kirstie cocked her head to one side and looked at her mother.

"Hmm." Sandy set off indoors with the heavy stack of plates. "One step at a time," she insisted. "We haven't even gotten a saddle on him yet."

Kirstie and Lisa glowered at Matt for spoiling the mood. Kirstie knew her mom was still worried about the two thousand dollars they'd paid for Rodeo Rocky, and was still having to consider the possibility of selling Yukon and her tiny foal to make up for the two thousand dollars she'd spent.

"So?" Matt widened his eyes and shrugged.

"Soon!" Kirstie answered back. She turned around and walked away, down the green bank to the edge of the creek, where she gazed across at the horses in the meadow. She could easily pick out Cadillac's white form from the rest in the twilight, and shadowing him was ugly-beautiful, faithful Crazy Horse. Then beyond them was pretty, dainty Johnny Mohawk, and beyond him the golden coat and pale blond mane of Kirstie's precious Lucky. Sure enough, at his side was Rocky. He was turned away from the herd, head up, staring at the wild slopes of Eagle's Peak, as if his mind was soaring up there, away from the ranch to the pine-tree wilderness in the quiet evening air.

Kirstie saw him and sighed.

"When?" Matt had followed her to the river's edge, and spoke quietly from behind. "It's time to saddle and ride him," he told her. "So when will it be?"

A saddle on the wild mustang's back. A metal bit in his mouth. Reins to hold him back. It was the big, big step.

"Tomorrow," she whispered. "I'll give it a try."

Yukon looked over the fence of the round pen as Kirstie chose a saddle and carried it out of the tack room. The mare's eight-day-old black foal skipped and bucked across the sandy ground on her spindly legs. Her large head with its white star wobbled up and down as she scampered across. Each day she grew a little bigger, a little steadier on her feet. And Yukon was a good mother, protecting her from the too-curious gaze of some of the ranch guests, standing over her when, tired out by playing and feeding, she folded her legs and took a nap in the sun.

Kirstie smiled at the mother and foal, hooked the heavy saddle over the corral fence, and then walked on to fetch Rocky.

"We have to sell something!" Matt had insisted over breakfast. He said he'd been working on some figures late the previous night, and he couldn't make them add up to show a profit unless they took the tough decision to sell at least one horse.

"I hear you," Sandy had said with a worried frown. "And I know it's not looking good right now. But maybe we'll hit lucky with a late booking. If we got in some extra guests, that would solve the cash flow problem."

"Yeah, and it would solve the problem if we sold the rodeo horse," Matt had said, looking pointedly at Kirstie. "We'd get our two thousand dollars back; end of story!"

Kirstie had deliberately turned her back on him, put on her fleece jacket to keep off the chill of the morning dew, and come out for Rocky's saddle.

Saddle equals rodeo. Rodeo equals ropes, loss of freedom, pain. She predicted the train of thought inside Rocky's head as she approached Red Fox Meadow. He would hate the sight of the polished leather and metal stirrups the moment he saw it. It would take all of Kirstie's calmness and courage to help him through this.

"Excuse me, Ma'am, can I get your horse for you?" Charlie's joking voice broke into her thoughts with the

70

phrase he and Hadley used on female ranch guests. He was riding across the meadow toward her with Cadillac and Crazy Horse in tow.

"Oh, hey Charlie!" She gave him a small grin. "Do you have time to watch me tack Rocky up?"

"When?" From his saddle, the wrangler watched the ex-rodeo stallion trot willingly to greet her.

She slipped a headcollar onto the bay horse and led him toward the gate, squinting into the sun that sat on the rim of the hills behind the cabins. "Right now?"

"Sure thing." Charlie said he would ask Hadley for a ten-minute break, and then join her at the round pen.

So Kirstie had Rocky inside the ring and was lunging him on a fifteen foot rein when Charlie joined her. "He noticed the saddle slung over the fence," she told him quietly. "I let him sniff at it for a while. He seemed OK about it, but I don't know how he'll be when I put it on his back."

"He'll be great," Charlie told her. "I'll take the rein while you fix his saddle."

She took a deep breath. It was now or never. As Charlie slowed the horse from a trot to a walk, then reined him to a standstill, she approached with the saddle.

"That's right, nice and easy," Charlie said softly, as Rocky's ears flicked and he bowed his head.

Kirstie lifted the heavy weight level with Rocky's shoulders. Her arms ached with the effort, but she didn't let the saddle drop straight down on the horse's back. Instead, she let him turn his head to look, waited until he'd agreed that it was OK to go ahead, then eased it onto the curve of his back. Gently, gently she lowered it until it rested comfortably in position.

"Easy, boy!" Charlie whispered. The lunge rein stayed relaxed in his hands.

"You're doing great!" Kirstie soothed. She didn't let Rocky see how keyed up she was as she lowered the cinch, took the strap under his belly and brought it up the other side. Before the horse knew it, the buckles were fastened and stirrups lowered.

Rocky shifted under the new weight and the feel of the tight cinch. But he didn't seem to seriously object.

"Good boy!" Now she praised him and patted him, rubbed his neck and shoulders, made a great fuss. "Trot him around the ring while I fetch the bridle," she told Charlie, dashing to the tack room once more. As she unhooked a bridle from its peg, she saw Hadley and said he should come and watch. Then they bumped into Matt and Sandy in the yard. "Everyone come and see this!" Kirstie insisted, running back into the pen.

And now she was confident that Rocky would trust her with the rest of the tack. She might even be able to ride him. But she mustn't be too eager. Slow and easy, she told herself. Charlie grinned at her and she grinned back as she approached the horse.

"Now this bridle is just like a headcollar," she explained. "There's a metal bar that slides inside your mouth, and a few straps around your face. I fasten it real simple, and the reins go over your head, like so." Kirstie talked as she worked, conscious of her small audience standing at the gate.

Rocky shook his head and snorted. He felt the cold metal in his mouth; a strange sensation for the horse from the flat Wyoming plains. He turned to look at Kirstie with a big question mark in his eyes.

"This is so I can get up on your back," she told him, keeping her voice calm and cheerful. "Sure, I know it's a whole lot of fancy stuff and you'd let me on without it, but it helps me stay up there, believe me!"

"Try riding him," Charlie urged.

Kirstie glanced at her mom, who hesitated, then nodded.

So Kirstie slid her left hand down Rocky's neck and took hold of a bunch of coarse black mane along with the slim rein straps. She bent her left leg and hooked her foot into the stirrup, then, holding onto the curved back of the saddle with her right hand, she heaved herself off the ground and slung her free leg over.

"Yes!" Charlie breathed.

She was in the saddle, looking down at Rocky's broad shoulders and long, coppery brown neck. He was skittering sideways, dancing a little, but not seriously misbehaving.

"That's excellent, Kirstie!" Sandy called across the pen.

"Cool." Matt nodded his approval.

Hadley said nothing, as usual.

But as the old wrangler called Charlie to help him saddle the other horses in the corral, Kirstie could tell that even

73

Hadley was impressed by the progress she'd made with the wild horse.

Taking a deep breath of fresh mountain air, she tightened the reins and tilted her heels down in the broad stirrups. Settled and balanced, safely astride, now she felt ready for whatever Rodeo Rocky might throw at her.

7

"You make the right things easy for the horse and the wrong things hard," Sandy Scott told Kirstie. They were working with Rodeo Rocky in the round pen five days after the stallion had been successfully saddled and ridden. It was late evening, a time when tiny bats flitted overhead and the mule deer wandered down from the high slopes, stalked by shadowy gray coyote with their telltale howling cry.

"Meaning?" Kirstie left off teaching Rocky to respond to the reins and walked him quietly over to where her mom stood.

Sandy tilted her hat back and began her explanation. "Well, you make the right things easy by making them fun. When Rocky obeys the rein to the right, you rub his shoulder and scratch his neck, do all the things he likes."

"And if he gets it wrong?" Kirstie couldn't imagine that her mother was telling her to hit or punish him in any way.

"You hold back the praise and the fun. A horse likes the games you play with him when he gets it right. He likes them so much; it feels bad for him when it doesn't happen. So next time, he'll try to understand what you're asking him and do his best to get it right."

"But I don't have fun with him until he does?" Kirstie set off with Rocky around the pen to try the reining technique once more. This time, the horse responded well, so she leaned forward to praise and pat him.

"That's really good." Sandy too was pleased. She stood back and watched Kirstie work on until the light got too bad. Then together they unsaddled Rocky and led him out to the meadow, where Lucky stood at the gate waiting for him, his pale mane and tail highlighted in the deepening dusk. Kirstie let Rocky loose and the two horses greeted each other, then loped the length of the field.

"Happy?" Sandy asked Kirstie as they walked back to the ranch.

"Yep." They crossed the bridge, noticing the lights go on in the cabins, hearing Hadley play his harmonica in the bunkhouse doorway. "How about you?"

"Yep," Sandy replied.

"So can I ride Rocky on the trail?" Kirstie waited for the reply for what seemed like an age. She felt he was about ready to try and begin work as a ranch horse, but would Sandy see it that way?

Her mom stepped onto the ranch house porch, took off her hat and shook her hair loose. "Why not give Lisa a call?"

Kirstie ran ahead of her. "Mom, what kind of answer is that? I was asking about trail riding Rocky!"

"Sure." A smile played about Sandy's lips. "That's why I said you should give Lisa a call."

"Huh? What's the connection?"

The smile broadened. "I'm thinking Lucky and Rocky. They like to be together. And that makes me think you and Lisa. You get on pretty well, too. So if Lisa can make it tomorrow, and she wants to ride Lucky . . ."

". . . That means I could ride Rocky and we could all go out on the trail!" Kirstie jumped in. "Great idea, Mom!"

Flinging her baseball cap down on the porch-swing and dashing into the house to grab the phone before Sandy could have second thoughts, she went ahead with the arrangements for Rocky's biggest test of all.

"Excuse me, Ma'am, can I get your horse for you?" Charlie came up behind Lisa as she stood in line in the corral the next day. He grinned sideways at Kirstie.

Lisa turned around. "Hey, Charlie, it's me!"

"Wow!" The wrangler stepped back in mock surprise.

Kirstie jerked Lisa's arm to pull her out of line. "He's fooling. Come on, we're going with Hadley on the advanced ride."

It was all arranged. Lisa's mom had driven her daughter up before opening time at the diner. Lisa had arrived in new jeans and boots, wearing a native American necklace made from leather and tiny turquoise, white and black beads. "We're not going on a fashion shoot!" Kirstie had cried. "We're trail riding up to Bear Hunt Overlook, remember!"

That morning she'd pulled on an old check shirt belonging to Matt. It was faded and torn. Her jeans were worn at the knees and rolled up at the bottom. "It looks like those are mine too," her brother had grumbled as she wolfed down a breakfast of waffles and chocolate sauce.

"Don't mess up your new jeans!" Bonnie called to Lisa from the old Ford pickup truck as she drove away. The warning had drifted off on the breeze.

And now Kirstie was hurrying her friend over to the post where Lucky and Rocky were tethered because Hadley was ready to head his group of experienced riders out on the trail. There was no time to talk or worry about the ride ahead as they quickly mounted and followed the line of guests out of the corral and over the wooden bridge.

As the horses' hooves clattered, then came back onto solid ground, Lisa saw that Rocky was edgy and urged Lucky ahead. "He'll follow if Lucky leads," she called over her shoulder, urging the palomino into a trot and sitting neatly in the saddle.

Sure enough, Rocky picked up his pace, ears forward, concentrating on Lucky, as Hadley took a trail that led to one side of Hummingbird Rock, and on through Fat Man's Squeeze to the giant overlook beyond.

Kirstie took care to praise him for settling down. Instead of pulling at the reins and dancing sideways, he went willingly, picking up his feet and choosing the surest, safest way through the bushes and between the rocks. Soon he was confident enough to put on speed and stride out alongside Lucky, catching up with the rest of the group just as the head wrangler was instructing them to split up and lope on past Hummingbird Rock.

"Meet up at the bunch of ponderosa pines," he told the visitors. "After that, there's a steep climb until we get to a narrow gulley. We do that part of the ride together, OK?"

The half-dozen riders nodded and went their separate ways, giving their horses their heads and loping across country. They ducked and dodged branches, jumped fallen logs, sometimes staying in the saddle by grasping the horn and clinging on as the horse charged ahead.

"You think you can do this?" Hadley stayed behind to ask Kirstie and Lisa.

They nodded and reined their horses around to face the slope. Kirstie could feel Rocky's eagerness as he scented the keener air blowing from the mountain tops. When she squeezed his sides and let him go on, he surged away without even waiting for Lucky.

And they were off up the hill, thundering across the

ground. Kirstie ducked to miss an overhanging branch, swept by the side of another, and swayed in the saddle as Rocky swerved around a rock. Behind her, she could hear Lisa and Lucky close on their heels. Ahead, the dude riders had fanned out, each taking a different track to the finishing point by the pines. Like them, she arrived breathless and pleased.

"OK?" Lisa checked with Kirstie. The wind had blown her hair into unruly curls, the pretty necklace was crooked, but she had a huge grin on her face.

"Great. Rocky is fantastic!" She kept her voice low in case Lucky got upset and jealous. "And so are you too!" she told him. The two horses jostled in the shadow of the pine trees, then got into line as Hadley checked that everyone was there.

"We're gonna go through the Squeeze," he reminded them. "It's a gulley between two cliffs. Some of the horses don't like it, but you let them know who's giving the orders and they'll do it, no problem."

Kirstie knew the place. It was only wide enough for one horse at a time. To either side, the pink-gray granite rocks rose sheer and bare. As she held back and set Rocky on the trail last in the line, she began to worry, and her edginess was picked up by the smart horse.

"OK?" Lisa turned to check again.

Rocky was falling behind, shaking his head and flattening his ears.

"He doesn't like the cliffs," Kirstie answered. The

shadows from the tall rocks had closed in, and by this time the first riders had entered the Squeeze. "Tight spaces remind him of the rodeo chutes, I guess!"

"You want to turn back?"

"No. Let's try," she decided. How would it look if she and Lisa rode back to the ranch early? They would have to give Sandy and Matt the reason, and admit that Rocky wasn't going to make the grade as a working horse after all. Not yet, at any rate, and time was short.

So they rode on into the gulley, Lucky stepping out first as if there was no problem, picking his way over the rocky ground, sure-footed and confident as ever.

Rocky watched him every inch of the way. Where Lucky went, he could go too. Though he was tense and tight, he battled with his fear and went on.

"Easy, boy!" Kirstie soothed him with her voice and helped him along. The track narrowed and the rocks rose high to either side. Inside the Squeeze the light was gloomy, the air damp, all sound deadened.

But Rocky made it through. Hating every second, flinching as he went, he came out the other side to join the group. Hadley gave Kirstie a sharp, questioning look. She nodded, and without a word Rocky carried on.

"Rocky's a grade A student!" Lisa sighed happily as the riders tethered their horses to tree branches on Bear Hunt Overlook. The others went ahead to sit at the edge of the rock and take in the spectacular view down the valley during

81

their ten-minute break. "He just took his first exam and passed!"

Kirstie slid from the saddle and led Rocky to a vacant tree. The ride had taken more out of her than she was ready to admit. Her mind had been full of questions that she'd had to keep hidden, and the effort of telling Rocky not to worry, of keeping him on the trail with the other horses, had been hard on her. Now she felt pleased but tired, glad of the rest as she unhitched Rocky's tether rope and began to tie it to a low branch.

She was hurrying with the slipknot in order to retrace her steps across the flat top of the overlook to rejoin Lisa and Lucky, when a sudden noise in a bush on a steep slope to the side of the tree stopped her. Rocky heard it too, froze and stared up at the rustling branches.

"Come on, Kirstie!" Lisa yelled, wanting to climb to the top of the overhang and join the rest of the group.

Her voice must have alarmed the creature crouched under the bush. The leaves shook, the branches parted, and out crawled a gray, silent shape.

"Coyote!" Kirstie cried. She recognized the wild dog in an instant, with its thick fur and long, bushy tail, its thin, pointed muzzle and slanting amber eyes that stared down at them from the rocky slope.

Before she knew it, the startled animal had crept free of the bush and started to advance. It was coming at her, lip curled back to show vicious canine teeth, a low growl deep in his throat.

"Get out of there!" Lisa yelled. Then she called for Hadley. "Kirstie's in trouble!" she cried. "Coyote!"

Shock rooted Kirstie to the spot. She heard her friend's cries, but the creature's white fangs mesmerized her. She couldn't move, couldn't defend herself, as it crouched above her head, ready to leap.

It snarled and launched itself, flying through the air in a rush of gray and fawn fur; it would have landed on top of her, its teeth snapping and tearing, if it hadn't been for Rocky. The horse's head went up, he pulled at the half-tied rope and broke free. Then he whirled around to rear up between the coyote and Kirstie, so that the creature came down on his back, across the saddle. The sudden movement knocked the coyote sideways onto the ground at Rocky's feet, where it lay winded.

"Don't move!" Hadley ordered Kirstie, seeing what had happened and running from the overhang with Lisa. "Let the horse handle it!"

She felt her legs shaking, her heart beating fast. Rocky had reared up again, intent on bringing his hooves down on the coyote, which rolled clear at the last instant. The mustang reared again, and the wild dog writhed and staggered to its feet. Tail between its legs, head hanging, it crept away before the flailing hooves landed a second time.

Then Hadley was there, taking hold of Rocky's tether, making sure that the coyote had had enough and really was on its way. He watched it slink into the brushwood in the shadow of the rocks.

"How's Rocky? Is he OK?" Kirstie came to all of a sudden, as if a hypnotist had clicked his fingers and released her from a spell. Shock made her body tremble from head to foot.

The old wrangler held the horse tight, checking his back and haunches for scratches and bites. "There's not a mark on him," he confirmed.

"Wow, you were lucky!" Lisa gasped.

Kirstie shook her head. "Not lucky. It was down to Rocky. He saved me!"

She leaned weakly against him, stroking his neck while he lowered his head and turned toward her.

"Sure thing," Hadley agreed. He pulled his hat low over his forehead and gave no other sign that a crisis had been narrowly avoided in all the time they were at Bear Hunt

Overlook, nor during the ride back to the ranch. It was only when they were unsaddling the horses in the corral and Sandy Scott hurried over to find out how Rocky had coped with his first trail ride that the wrangler let anything slip.

He was taking the bay stallion's heavy saddle from Kirstie and carrying it into the tack room when he crossed paths with the anxious ranch owner.

"Well?" Sandy demanded.

Kirstie watched Hadley's face. She held her breath and prayed for him to give the right answer. The old man's narrowed eyes and straight, thin-lipped mouth gave nothing away.

"You got yourself a good horse," he said at last with the ghost of a smile. "He's worth every cent you paid."

8

"OK, we can relax!" Matt announced. He came off the phone with good news for Sandy. "I've been speaking with a guy called Jerry Santos. He's staying with his wife and three kids at Lone Elm Trailer Park. Lennie told him about this place and now he wants to book a cabin and a riding holiday for the whole family, starting tomorrow!"

It was a week after Kirstie had started riding Rocky out on the trails, when the mustang had first won Hadley's approval. Ever since the day with the coyote, the old wrangler had insisted on taking Rocky and Kirstie out with his advanced group to show Rocky the most difficult rides and to test out his temperament to the limit. As a further test, both the head wrangler and Charlie had also ridden him. So far, so good, Hadley had reported to his boss. The bay horse had taken every overlook, every cascading waterfall, every challenge that the mountain trails provided easily in his stride.

As yet, there had been no decision to put a guest rider in Rocky's saddle, but confidence in him was growing. Kirstie felt that it wouldn't be long now before the ex-rodeo horse became a full working member of the Half-Moon Ranch team.

And now the cash flow problem caused by Sandy's impulse buy seemed to be easing too. Extra, last minute guests recommended by Lisa's grandfather would bring in much needed money, and even Matt was smiling as he gave them the news.

"Great! So we get to keep Yukon and her foal?" Kirstie walked out of the house with her brother and mom, passing the round pen as they made their way to the corral. Inside the fenced ring, the tiny, coal-black horse skipped and pranced in the early morning sun.

Sandy nodded, then paused. "Time to give her a name?" she suggested. It was all the answer Kirstie needed.

Stepping on the bottom rung of the fence, she leaned in and smiled at the foal's antics and at Yukon contentedly nipping hay from a net on the far side of the pen. "Your turn to choose," she said to Matt.

"A name for the foal?" He was still checking figures in

his head, not concentrating on the high kicks and wobbles, the dancing and prancing of the youngster. "You choose," he told Kirstie absentmindedly, then walked on.

Just then, the little horse tried out a kick with her back legs. She churned up a cloud of dust in the sandy pen. The dust got into her nose, she shook her head and sneezed.

"Pepper," Kirstie decided with a broad grin. "From now on, that's her name!"

"*All* the horses can stay!" she told Lisa the next morning.

While Matt and Sandy were busy with the usual Sunday transfer of guests from the ranch to the Denver airport, the girls had decided to ride out along Meltwater Trail to Miners' Ridge. It was a chance for a quiet, peaceful trek without having to think about visitors or stick closely to the trails.

"For a while back there, I was afraid things weren't working out," Kirstie confessed. They'd reached the ridge, with Dead Man's Canyon below and a track up through the ponderosa pines to Lisa's grandfather's trailer park. Rocky took the ridge without faltering, despite the steep drop to one side. He looked keenly at the mounds of waste rock from the old goldmine now overgrown with grass, decided they were OK, and walked steadily on. Not even the rush of water over the rocks and the loud, foaming cascade into the canyon put him off, as Kirstie led the way.

"I knew Rocky would make the grade!" Lisa said cheerfully. "Thanks to you, of course!"

"And to Charlie." Kirstie reminded her of the young wrangler's help. She breathed deeply and relaxed in the saddle as they left the ridge behind. "How about calling on your grandpa?" she suggested.

"Sure." Lisa brought Lucky up alongside Rocky, and for a while they walked without talking. Their silence brought out the mule deer from the bushes and long, dry grass, which grew on the open slopes. The slender, large-eared deer wandered by in groups of five or six, the cautious does leading their fawns and year-old young to better grazing land below the ridge.

"Lennie made Matt's day yesterday," Kirstie told Lisa, once they reached the more level, broader track that led to Lone Elm. "He's sending some people from the trailer park to the ranch. Matt's had dollar signs in his eyes all morning!"

Lisa grinned. "I heard that. Grandpa says the Santos family drove all the way from New Jersey in a big recreational vehicle to take their vacation in the Rockies. But I guess they've had it up to here with roughing it. Now they want a week in a nice cabin with a fireplace and a porch, and someone to do the cooking and the dishes!"

"That sounds good to me, too!" Kirstie laughed. Up ahead she could already see the entrance to the trailer park, and beyond that the neat log-built reception building nestled under the tall, solitary elm tree from which the park took its name.

"Hey, that could be Jerry Santos and family moving out right now!" Lisa spotted a high-sided, silver motor home parked by the side of the office. It gleamed in the sunlight;

a giant vehicle decked out with big steel fenders, ladders onto the roof, and windows with fancy blinds. In the cab sat a woman and three small kids, and down by the office door stood a man in T-shirt and shorts. "Let's go see!"

Quick off the mark, Lucky broke into a trot and then a lope along the smooth track. Less eager to break the peaceful spell of their mountain ride, Kirstie held Rocky back for a few seconds. She saw more deer and stopped to watch a buck rub his beautiful antlers against a pine tree, listening to the scrape and hollow rattle of horn against bark. In the undergrowth behind, a young, pale brown doe with huge, dark eyes darted from bush to bush.

Glancing ahead, Kirstie saw that Lisa and Lucky had already reached the entrance to the trailer park. She decided to give Lisa time to say hello to her grandpa before she caught up to them. But then she frowned. The fair-haired man in shorts was stepping toward the silver motor home and climbing up into the cab as Lisa arrived. He was turning on the engine. The giant vehicle was starting to move out of the park.

"Lisa, watch out for Lucky!" Kirstie yelled. Her voice was drowned by the engine.

Now she had other things to worry about. The motor home crawled through the exit, beneath the overhead sign that Lennie Goodman had erected only that spring. Thirty feet long, reflecting the sun's rays, engine growling, it advanced onto the track.

"For goodness' sake!" she muttered. Didn't the driver

have enough sense to wait until she and Rocky had ridden by? Though broader than the steep mountain trails, the road couldn't fit both motor home and horse. And anyway, Rocky was beginning to act up.

He saw the square front of the tall cab, the gleaming metal grille, the flash of sunlight reflected on glass, the movement of passengers inside. For a few moments, Rocky stood stock still.

Kirstie tightened the reins. "Back up!" she whispered. If Rocky would pull back a few feet, she could guide him up a side track, out of the way of the slowly advancing motor home. "Come on, Rocky, let's get out of here!"

No way was the driver going to stop, she realized. Maybe he thought he had the right of way in his huge motor home, and expected a mere horse and rider to automatically give way. Or maybe he just didn't realize he was giving her a problem. In any case, he kept right on coming.

She felt the mustang flinch. Instead of backing to safety, he chose to advance with edgy, uneven strides. Kirstie pulled on the reins. "Come on, Rocky, what's going on?" Why wouldn't he do as he was told?

He stopped. His head was up, ears flat; the old, angry signs. And every muscle was tense, every nerve on edge as he skittered across the dirt road, defying the oncoming driver.

The man at the wheel must have seen the horse by now. He was a hundred yards away and still creeping forwards. Either he was mean or stupid. "Stop!" Grasping the reins in one hand, Kirstie made a firm signal with the other.

91

No response. The giant vehicle kept on coming. There was a roar, a cloud of black fumes from the exhaust, a swing off the road into the gravel and brushwood, as if the driver had momentarily lost control. A screech of brakes, the churn of loose stones under the massive wheels; the inexperienced driver fought to bring the tilting motor home back onto level ground.

"Easy, boy!" Kirstie knew deep down that she was losing him. He was ignoring her voice, the touch of the reins. His muscles were bunched, his head straining. Still she tried to get him back.

But it was no good. With a toss of his head, Rocky rested back deep onto his haunches, then threw himself forward in a terrific buck. Kirstie flew with him in a high arc, grabbing the saddle horn as she went, legs flying from the stirrups, head jerked back in a sudden whiplash movement. Her hat flew off, and her hair fell loose as she clung to the saddle and felt Rocky's back feet land with a thudding jolt.

It was then, much too late, that the driver must have realized she was in deep trouble. He put his foot on the brake and trundled to a halt. The motor home hissed, spouted out blue smoke, and then sat motionless astride the track.

With Kirstie still clinging tight, trying to slide her feet back into the stirrups and regain hold of the reins, Rocky arched his back and stamped his feet. A huge fear had him in its grip. His head went up again, his mane whipping against her arms. Then he reared and twisted, throwing her

back and sideways. She held on, and felt the bunched fury of his muscles.

Then there were footsteps running down the road, two figures appeared from behind the stationary motor home. Kirstie glimpsed Lisa and Lennie Goodman coming to help. But Rocky spun away, rearing once, twice, three times. She was flung backwards and forwards, biting her tongue hard as her jaw fell open then snapped shut with the violent rise and fall. There was blood in her mouth; a salty, metallic taste, but no time to feel pain.

The mustang whirled, turned and reared. It was the wild Rocky; the frightened, crazy Rocky of the rodeo. An old fear had exploded in his brain, making him fight to be rid of his rider, to rage up the mountain to freedom once more.

"Hang on, Kirstie!" Lisa cried.

Kirstie gripped the horn, pressed her legs against the mustang's flanks, her head jerked this way and that. Already dizzy and weak, she felt him veer to the side and charge at the steep slope that bordered the road. There was a boulder in his path that he would smash against unless he took off and jumped . . . she soared with him and landed, and felt him thunder on up the rough hillside.

Rocky had jumped clear of the road and charged up the steep slope, between trees and rocks, in a mad frenzy to be away from the terrifying, hissing truck. Reins flapping, stirrups crashing against his sides, and with Kirstie slumped forward in the saddle, he raced on.

Tall tree trunks flashed by, branches whipped against

her, and she cried out. She recognized the ridge that Rocky had reached and the drop into Dead Man's Canyon. There was blood trickling from her mouth, a throbbing sensation as the pain set in. And still she must duck and sway out of reach of the blurred branches, gasp for breath and stay in the saddle . . . not fall . . . not land on the dangerous rocks or be flung over the edge of the cliff down the sheer drop into the canyon . . .

Rocky swerved to avoid a low bush. He stumbled against loose rocks, and fell to his knees.

Kirstie felt herself thrown forward so hard that she lost hold of the saddle horn. Rocky was down and she was flying through the air. The world turned and spun. Her shoulder crashed against a rock, there was a shooting pain in her neck and head, then blackness, silence . . . nothing.

"Kirstie . . .? Come on, wake up! Kirstie . . . please!"

She came around from a dim, distant world, out of a dark tunnel, away from the silent shadows. She opened her eyes to trees, sky, and Lisa's anxious face peering down at her.

"Where's Rocky?" she moaned. Her mouth felt like a dark cave in which the hollow words rolled.

"Never mind the horse. Are you OK?" Lisa knelt by her side, afraid to touch her.

"What happened? Where's Rocky?"

"He threw you off, remember? You landed badly, you've been out cold for more than ten minutes!"

"But where is he?" Struggling to raise herself onto her elbows, she turned her stiff neck to search the empty hillside.

Gently Lisa wiped the blood from her face. "He threw you, and then ran off. Grandpa took Lucky and went for help. You lie still until the others get here."

Kirstie shook her head and struggled to sit up. "I need to find him. Which way did he go?" But the pain in her shoulder was bad; her head swam and she sank back down.

"Forget about Rocky," Lisa whispered. "You're hurt. You're not going anywhere."

The trees shook their golden leaves down on her. They floated and drifted onto her face. She felt their feathery touch . . .

"Kirstie?" Lisa's echoing voice broke through.

Her eyelids fluttered open again. *Forget about Rocky.* That was Lisa. *He threw you, then ran off. Forget about Rocky. Forget about him* . . . She tried to focus on the trees over her head, but she heard the beat of hooves on rock, saw a dream horse race along the ridge. *Forget about Rocky.* That's what they would all say when they got here, her mom, Hadley, and Matt. *He's a problem horse. He'll never be any good.*

Their voices floated in her head. It throbbed and spun. The voices judged the mustang and sentenced him over and over again: *Forget him.* From now on, she knew that this was how it would be.

9

The doctor came from San Luis and reassured Sandy Scott that Kirstie's shoulder was badly bruised but not broken. The cut on her tongue would also heal itself in time.

It wasn't the cuts and bruises that mattered. Forced to lie in bed while her mom showed the doctor downstairs, Kirstie dismissed the minor injuries she'd sustained when Rodeo Rocky threw her and fled up the mountain. What mattered was the damage to her dream that one day soon he would join the team of horses at Half-Moon Ranch. She stared out of the open window at distant Eagle's Peak, nursing her shattered pride and hope.

"It could've been worse, I guess." Lisa slid quietly into the room while the grown-ups talked over the accident in the ranch house kitchen. "No broken bones."

"Have they found Rocky?" Kirstie demanded.

"Your mom sent Hadley and Charlie out to look." Gazing awkwardly at the floor, Lisa found it hard to meet her friend's intense gaze.

"But they didn't find him yet?" She realized the runaway stallion could have traveled miles off the trails and beaten tracks into thick pine forests, or even above the snowline into the icy wastes of the high peaks of the Meltwater range.

"Nope. They took a two-way radio, so they'll call as soon as they've got news." Lisa glanced up and tried to smile. "How are you doing?"

"Fine." Kirstie stared hard at Lisa's flushed face.

"I heard the doc tell your mom you had to stay in bed in case you have a concussion."

"I'm fine! It's Rocky I'm worried about." Kirstie felt a long, embarrassed pause develop between them. "Do you know something you're not telling me?"

"Nope." Lisa's coloring was pale and freckled. When she lied, her face flushed bright red.

Kirstie sat up in bed, trying to catch snatches of conversation from downstairs. "What's going on down there? What are they saying?"

"I dunno. Grandpa's telling your mom about the accident.

He reckons Rocky went kind of crazy back there and you're lucky you weren't hurt real bad."

"Is that right?" She was all for getting straight out of bed and running down to the kitchen to put them right, until Lisa put out a hand to stop her.

"Wait till they've calmed down. Arguing won't do any good right now."

So Kirstie sat on the edge of the bed and gave her friend a rough time instead. "It's not Rocky who was crazy; it's that dumb driver! What on earth was he thinking; driving a giant truck at a horse like that? Doesn't he *know* that's the best way to spook any horse on this planet? Let alone one that's been through what Rodeo Rocky's been through!"

"You don't need to tell me!" Lisa pointed out when Kirstie finally paused for breath.

"Look, how can they blame Rocky? To him that motor home must've looked like the truck they used to drive him down from Wyoming! Big steel fenders, wide, flashing windscreen, loud engine . . ." To Kirstie it was obvious. "Rocky sees this monster machine coming down the track toward him, and he thinks, no way! Once was enough. He's not gonna stick around until men with ropes come and grab him again. He's been there before!"

"Sure, Kirstie, I hear what you're saying." Going to look out of the window at the doctor's car driving out under the Half-Moon Ranch sign, Lisa tried once more to get a word in. "And maybe you're right about Rocky having a good reason not to like these giant trucks, but . . ."

"*But*, nothing!" She felt her heart pounding with a fierce desire to defend the horse. "Rocky was only doing what any horse in his right mind would have done!"

Lisa sighed, opened her mouth to speak, and then changed her mind.

"Go ahead!" Nursing her elbow in the palm of her hand to ease the pain in her shoulder, Kirstie joined her at the window. She winced and frowned to see the very motor home they'd been talking about parked on a flat piece of land beyond the bridge over the creek. It looked like the Santos family had arrived for their week's stay at the ranch. The sight of it made her stomach churn. "OK, Lisa, give it to me straight."

Lisa turned her gray eyes to meet Kirstie's blue ones. "I guess you have to know."

"Know what?" She heard the door swing open, saw Matt stride out across the yard, heard her mom's footsteps treading back and forth in the hallway at the bottom of the stairs.

At last Lisa spoke the difficult words. "Sandy's gonna blame Rocky, whatever you say. It figures. She's really worried about you. And if Grandpa tells her the horse went crazy, no way is she gonna let you ride him again . . .!"

"Not let me ride Rocky?" The idea struck Kirstie like a physical blow.

Lisa chewed her lip and nodded. "You'd better believe it," she murmured. "And that's even if they do track him down and get him back to Half-Moon Ranch!"

"I swear, Mom, it won't happen again!" Kirstie pleaded like she'd never pleaded before.

It was Monday morning, before the wranglers set off from the corral with the groups of new visitors. Hadley and Charlie had returned empty-handed the night before, reporting that there was no sign of Rodeo Rocky in any of the predictable places. They'd ridden through Dead Man's Canyon, and as far as Eden Lake, where they knew the runaway stallion would have found good grass for grazing. But there wasn't a hoof-mark anywhere to show the path he'd taken.

Now Kirstie was confined to the ranch house to help her heal, and though Lisa had promised to call and keep her company, a long, empty day stretched ahead.

"Give me a guarantee." Sandy spoke quietly but firmly. "Give me a one hundred per cent promise that, if we do track him down and bring him back, Rocky is gonna be a safe ride!"

Kirstie took a sharp breath through her nose. She tried to frame the words, to explain that the incident with the motor home had been a one-time thing.

In the tense silence, Sandy turned away. "You can't. Nobody can."

Kirstie stepped across her path, blocking the door before she went out onto the porch to collect her hat and set off on the day's ride. "Look at it this way. There are no roads here on the ranch land; only trails for horses. So, if Rocky is spooked by trucks because of what he went through earlier this summer, what we do is make sure he doesn't go near any roads. No roads: no trucks, see!" Her voice cracked, and her eyes shone with tears as she spread her hands to plead even harder than before. "No trucks: no problem!"

Sandy shook her head. "Kirstie, don't!"

"Why not?" To her, it was a life or death issue. No way could they give up on Rocky.

"Because I already made up my mind. It's too risky." Gently Sandy pushed past and picked up her hat.

"So?" Once more, Kirstie stepped across her path. "What are you gonna do? Just leave Rocky up there in the mountains?" How long would he survive among dangerous coyotes and mountain lions?

"Nope." Sandy avoided looking at Kirstie as she put on her Stetson and called across the yard to Matt to say that she was on her way. "As your brother just pointed out, there's two thousand dollars' worth of mustang out there somewhere. Hadley and Charlie will ask the other ranchers for help. There's gonna be a big search party tonight. We'll find him, you bet."

Kirstie took this in. She should have been relieved, but somehow she wasn't. "Then what?" she demanded from the top step of the porch. Her mom was striding away, not looking back.

"I called the sale barn in San Luis," she replied, her voice muffled as she hurried off. "We send Rocky to the auction at dawn tomorrow!"

"All you have to do is saddle Lucky for me!" Kirstie begged Lisa for help when her friend arrived in her grandpa's pickup truck. "I can't lift the weight of it with this shoulder the way it is!"

"No way!" Lisa backed out of the bedroom onto the landing. She put both hands in front of her to ward off Kirstie's pleas.

"Please! I'll do anything you want in return! Just this one little favor, Lisa, *please*!" All morning she'd sat by the bedroom window planning this, waiting for Lisa to show up.

"It's not a little favor, it's a mega, mega one! What's your mom gonna say if I let you do this?" She backed down the stairs shaking her head hard.

"I won't say a word, I promise. Your story is, you got here and I was already gone. The whole thing was my doing!"

"Uh-oh!" Lisa pointed out that Sandy Scott would know there was no way Kirstie could have saddled Lucky alone. "Besides, I wouldn't do it anyway. It's too risky."

"Since when has taking a risk become a problem?" Kirstie had struggled into her clothes before Lisa had arrived. Now she was pulling on her boots and following her friend downstairs. "We always take risks, don't we?"

"The doc said to stay in bed, remember!"

"That was yesterday. That was before I knew they planned to send Rocky to the sale barn!"

Lisa went on backing out across the hallway onto the porch. "OK, so say I saddle Lucky for you. You ride out on a trail looking for Rocky. What then?"

Seeing that she was weakening, Kirstie ran forward and grabbed her eagerly by the arm. "I made a plan! I'm trusting Lucky to track Rocky down. Lucky has got this kind of thing with him . . . you know, a . . . connection!"

Slowly Lisa nodded. "You reckon he'll find him, wherever he ran to?"

"Yeah! Horses can hear and smell way, way better than we can. And Lucky's smart. He thinks like Rocky thinks; kind of wild and clever. It won't take him long."

"Ouch!" Lisa pulled her arm away. "Then what?" she demanded.

"Then . . ." Kirstie hesitated. This was the part of the plan she wanted to keep to herself. "You don't want to know, Lisa. You really don't want to know!"

"If you don't tell me, no way will I help you!" Hurt that Kirstie wouldn't confide in her, Lisa drew back.

Kirstie's shoulders sank, she sighed. "Let's just say it's something I've got to do."

"So Rocky doesn't get sent to the auction?" Lisa frowned and stared hard at Kirstie's troubled face.

As she nodded, she felt hot tears come to her eyes. "It's gonna break my heart, believe me."

"And it's a secret?" Lisa whispered.

Another nod. She brushed the tears away and held her head up. "Trust me, Lisa."

There was a long, long silence. Then the red-haired girl broke away and across the yard toward the bridge. "Wait here," she yelled over her shoulder as she broke into a run.

"You go to the tack room. I'll bring Lucky in from the meadow!"

Kirstie was breaking every rule there was to break. The doc had said no riding for a few days, and here she was taking Lucky out along Meltwater Trail. Her mom had told her to give up on the problem rodeo horse, and that was something she just wasn't ready to do.

Giving up on Rocky and sending him in a dark horse trailer along the rough road to San Luis was the worst kind of betrayal. Worse than death for the wild, free-spirited stallion.

And Kirstie loved that horse. She loved him for his copper-coated beauty, his strength and willpower, and because of the way he'd learned to trust.

So she followed the track past waterfalls and fast-running streams, through Fat Man's Squeeze to Miners' Ridge, to the point where she and Lisa had left the official trail and bushwhacked over to the trailer park the day before.

Lucky took it easy, his trot smooth and gentle, as if he knew that Kirstie's shoulder hurt and this was the reason she sat stiff in the saddle, trusting him to pick his way through trees and rocks.

"Your mom will never forgive me if anything bad happens," Lisa had whispered as she'd tacked Lucky up and helped Kirstie into the saddle. Her face had been pale and strained as she'd stood by the corral fence and watched her leave.

Kirstie had managed to smile back at her. "You weren't even here!" she'd murmured.

And now she and Lucky had reached the spot where the Santos's motor home had spooked Rocky. There were the tire marks up ahead, where Jerry Santos had driven the giant vehicle off the track, and here were the scuffs and hoofprints where Rocky had reared and bucked. His track led across the dirt road, over a jagged rock and on up the hill.

Setting Lucky to follow the trail, Kirstie glanced over her shoulder to check that there was no one around. One way was the entrance to Lennie Goodman's trailer park. In the other direction was the empty road she'd just traveled. For a moment she felt Lucky hesitate and flick his ears as if he'd picked up a sound. Was it Rocky? Was the runaway horse standing quietly in that dark clump of pine trees, or behind that tall rock? Kirstie urged the palomino to investigate.

But no; that was too much to hope. The noise that had alerted Rocky must have been a deer or even a mountain lion. A cougar stalking through the bushes would make the palomino pay attention, that was for sure.

So Kirstie turned him away from possible danger and took a track away from the trailer park toward Eden Lake, high in the mountains.

This was a hunch worth following, but only a hunch. The lake, at eight thousand feet, was surrounded on three sides by massive rock faces. It was a natural cul-de-sac, but the approach provided plenty of good grass on the open slope. Rocky could find food, water from the crystal clear lake, and shelter from the wind in the lee of the mountains. Instinct might have led him there for the night.

Lucky too seemed to think it was a good decision. He picked up his pace as they left behind the last signs of civilization; a trailer nestling in the pine trees at the edge of the trailer park. His head was up and he wanted to lope, but Kirstie held him back because of the pain in her shoulder. She would keep him in a trot, posting out of the saddle to cut down the jarring sensation of the sitting trot.

They were cutting across country, about to cross the Eden Lake trail, and Kirstie was looking around to check that Hadley's group was nowhere in sight when Lucky suddenly skittered sideways, then stopped. He'd heard or seen something unusual, or else he'd picked up his rider's unease and the slightest thing had begun to spook him. "Come on, this isn't your problem," she said softly.

Lucky ignored her. He listened, turned his head down the trail, and waited.

Then Kirstie heard the sound of hooves coming along the trail. One horse only; approaching fast up the slope. Kirstie frowned and urged Lucky on into the covering of some nearby trees and rocks. Still he refused.

Then the horse rounded a bend and came into view. He was pale in the shadow of an overhanging rock, striding out so that his tail streamed behind him. His rider ducked to avoid a low branch, and when she sat up her hat flew back to reveal dark red curls.

"Lisa!" Kirstie called out. She reined Lucky around and went to meet her friend. "What the . . .?"

Lisa drew level, then pulled Cadillac up. "So?" she demanded, challenging Kirstie before she had time to object. "No way was I gonna let you ride up here by yourself!"

"You've been following me!" This explained the noises in the bushes by the trailer park, and Lucky's edginess.

"Yep." Lisa studied Kirstie's face. "You look pretty bad. How's the shoulder? No, don't answer that." She stared harder than ever. "So, where are we going?"

"We?" At first, Kirstie wouldn't show how glad she was to see Lisa. Finding Rocky was something she had to do alone. Yet she acknowledged the flood of relief she'd felt when she'd recognized both horse and rider. And she knew she didn't have the heart to send them back.

"We. You, me, Lucky and Cadillac." Lisa leaned forward to pat her horse's smooth, cream neck. Then she glanced up at Kirstie with a warm smile. "So, don't give me a hard time, OK? Where you go; Cadillac and I go, too!"

All morning they crisscrossed the wooded slopes, searching for the runaway horse. Lucky and Cadillac took the steep hills in their stride, pushing ahead to Eden Lake past creeks and waterfalls, across fast-running streams and up to clearings in the forest where Kirstie and Lisa could ride out onto flat overlooks to scan the valleys for signs of movement.

Beneath them, the land was empty and still. Once they caught a distant glimpse of one of the trail-riding groups; a

108

string of horses taking their riders along the beginners' Five Mile Creek Trail. Another time, a movement just below their overlook turned out to be a small family of mule deer. Kirstie swallowed her disappointment and headed on to the pasture by the lake.

As they drew near, the sun was high overhead and the heat building up. The sky was a dense blue, and there was no breeze. The girls rode into the bowl of land where the clear lake spread before them, into a world of green and blue silence.

Please! Kirstie prayed as she rode Lucky across the lush pasture toward the lake. *Even if Rocky isn't here, please give us a clue*!

A blue jay took off from a nearby tree and squawked across the sparkling water. High overhead a golden eagle soared on the wind currents.

Riding ahead, Lisa took Cadillac to the water's edge to let him drink. "Hey!" she called. "Kirstie, come look at these prints!"

Rocky had been to Eden Lake. The solo prints of hooves in the mud proved it. He wasn't here now; the great bowl of rocks was empty except for the birds. But he had visited the spot.

"How long ago?" Lisa asked.

"Not long. The track's fresh." Kirstie had dismounted to crouch beside the water. Lucky stood nearby, watching, listening.

109

"The prints head across the pasture toward that creek."
From the vantage point of her saddle, Lisa pointed to more
prints in the soft grass.

A stream flowed out of Eden Lake, across the flat
plateau toward a sudden drop. Kirstie recognized Crystal
Creek and Falls as a sight that took visitors' breaths away
when they first saw it from the trail below.

She also remembered that Hadley always gave a warning
for them to stay well clear of the tumbling, foaming mass of
water that slid over the edge and crashed between the rocks.
Though it looked cool, clear and inviting, the creek had
strong currents and dangerous banks. A horse tempted to
drink there could easily lose his footing in soft, quicksand-
like soil, then be dragged into the current and swept away.

Frowning to discover that Rocky had chosen such a risky
refuge, Kirstie remounted Lucky and began to ride toward
the creek. The aspen trees on the far bank whispered gently
in the breeze from the ice-capped peaks. The light danced on
their silvery leaves and dappled the shaded ground.

"Hey!" Lisa said softly. She pointed to the shadowy
bank.

Lucky stopped in the bright sunshine amidst a sweep of
green grass and blue columbines. Kirstie stared into the rip-
pling shadows. There was a copper glint, a horse emerging
from the trees. Bay and black, with the strange metallic tint.
Head up, raising himself onto his hind legs and whinnying
loudly, Rocky greeted Kirstie from the far bank of Crystal
Creek.

10

"What now?" Lisa's question was high and tense.

Kirstie drank in the sight of the magnificent mustang. As if in a daze, she rode Lucky toward the creek.

Lisa followed. "Come on, Kirstie, what's the plan?"

She stopped at the water's edge. The creek ran fast and deep. Not far to their left, it disappeared over a narrow ledge of rock in a thundering roar.

"So, we found him!" Lisa begged Kirstie to stop and explain. "You can't take Rocky back to the ranch, so what are we gonna do?"

"Me," she replied. "What am I gonna do? By myself. Alone."

Rocky came toward them and stood on the far bank, separated only by the creek.

"Kirstie, for goodness' sake!" Lisa could see she was in pain. Her face was pale, her jaw clenched as she let go of Lucky's reins and eased her shoulder.

Taking a deep breath, with her eyes still on Rocky, she answered quietly and firmly. "The plan's simple. I get up on Rocky and head him way out of here into the mountains. I ride him to Eagle's Peak and down into the next valley, where there are no ranches, no roads; just miles of forest."

"And?" Lisa rode Cadillac tight up beside her, following her gaze across the water to where Rocky stood.

"And nothing," Kirstie said. It was wild land without fences, with vast stretches of grass between the trees; pastures where deer grazed and horses roamed. Like Wyoming. Like the land the mustang knew best. She took a deep breath and told Lisa what was in her heart. "I'm going to set Rocky free!"

"But first you have to cross the creek!" Lisa pointed out the most obvious difficulty. "Forget that the pain in your shoulder is killing you. Ignore the fact that your mom is relying on getting her two grand back on the horse . . ."

"Don't think I haven't thought it through a hundred times." Kirstie shook her head and began to look for a safe place to cross. "But hey, have you got a better idea?"

The question silenced Lisa. She frowned and walked

Cadillac slowly along the bank of the stream. Opposite, Rocky had broken into an agitated trot. He ran a short distance by the water's edge, away from Crystal Falls, turned quickly and trotted back.

"OK, Lucky, we need to join Rocky." Kirstie edged her horse into the cold current. She felt him flinch as water lapped his knees. He hesitated, looking at Rocky, who was still trotting and wheeling around, whinnying now and pawing the ground.

"How deep is that water?" Lisa asked nervously. She watched a piece of sodden driftwood speed by, tumbling between jagged rocks, then swirling and disappearing under the surface.

Kirstie pressed Lucky's sides to order him on. "It doesn't matter; he can swim it, no problem."

"In that current?"

"He's strong. He can make it." She glanced across the creek. It was thirty feet wide at this point, and the far bank was low and flat enough for her horse to climb out easily. Only, Rocky seemed to be growing more upset at the place she'd chosen and to be warning Lucky against it. The mustang stamped and snorted, wheeled away and raced upstream. He took a slope and stopped on a ridge of rock, inviting them to follow.

With Lucky still only knee-deep in the water, Kirstie narrowed her eyes. "No, that's no good. It's too steep for us to get out there." Her chosen place was better, she decided. Once more she gave Lucky the signal to plunge in deep.

113

Reluctantly, straining at the reins, the palomino obeyed. He walked awkwardly into the current until, with a sudden jerk he was out of his depth and swimming. The water rose around Kirstie's legs and swamped the saddle. It closed over Lucky's shoulders. His legs paddled smoothly and strongly, resisting the force of the rushing current, carrying them across the creek to the far shore.

The ice-cold water pushed against Kirstie's legs. She was waist-deep and still in the saddle, leaning into the current to resist it, struggling with the pain of her injured shoulder. But Lucky was making progress; they'd gone beyond the halfway point and the bank was now only a short way off. Rocky had charged down from the ridge and stood quivering on a ledge of black rock some fifteen feet from the grassy spot where Lucky would land. He was still agitated; his ears were back, he tossed his head and stamped. Then, as Lucky found his feet touching the riverbed again, there was a sudden swirl and giant eddy. The current had switched. It threw Kirstie sideways, so that she had to cling to the drenched saddle horn to regain her balance.

"Hang on, Kirstie!" Lisa yelled from behind.

Up ahead, Rocky stopped his restless stamping and froze.

Kirstie hauled herself upright. "OK!" she whispered to Lucky. The worst was over. He could steady himself and walk on.

One step, two steps; unsteady because of the dangerous current, the palomino emerged from the creek. Three steps.

114

The bed of the stream was strewn with hidden rocks. Lucky staggered. On the black ledge, Rocky reared up, wheeled away, and came closer to the spot where Lucky was headed.

Breathless now with the effort of hanging on, dizzy from the rush and swirl of the current, Kirstie willed her horse forward. He rose out of the creek onto the grassy bank.

"Good boy, you made it!" There was a split second when she leaned forward to pat him. A moment when he lifted his first hoof and planted it on the reedy, squelching surface. The hoof sank into mud. It vanished. The soil oozed and sucked it under. Lucky tipped forward, lifted his other front leg, and planted it on the bank. It too sank knee-deep.

The horse was up to his knees in soft gray mud. He sank quickly to his shoulders, throwing Kirstie forward out of the saddle, over his head and onto the bank. She let go of the reins, rolled away, felt the mud suck at her, and kept on rolling until she could reach out and catch at the stirrup of the saddle Rocky was still wearing. The mustang stood just close enough, at the very edge of the treacherous swamp. He held firm as she rolled and caught the stirrup, took her weight, dragged her clear.

But Lisa was crying out a warning that Lucky was still sinking. She crouched on the far bank, ignoring two figures that had ridden across the flat meadow from the direction of Eden Lake and were flinging themselves out of their saddles at the water's edge. "Kirstie, get a rope around Lucky's neck, quick as you can! He's going under!"

Without thinking, Kirstie staggered to her feet and unhitched the lead rope coiled and hitched to the side of Rocky's saddle. As she ran back to the edge of the swamp, she tied a noose in one end. Then she aimed the rope and threw.

Eight or ten feet away, the palomino strove to keep his head and shoulders clear of the mud, which sucked and oozed at him, dragging him down. His eyes rolled wildly, he lashed his head from side to side, but his feet found nothing solid and his struggles only made him sink more quickly.

The noose landed wide of the palomino. Kirstie groaned and drew the rope back, gathered it and aimed again. This time, it snaked through the air and over Lucky's head.

"Neat!" a voice called from the far bank.

Kirstie glanced up and had time to recognize Hadley and Charlie as the figures that had raced across the meadow. Now Hadley was yelling instructions.

"Tighten the rope!"

She nodded and stepped back until it was taut.

"OK, now tie the end around Rocky's saddle horn!" The wrangler gave smooth, clear orders. "Done that?"

With trembling, muddy fingers, she did as she was told.

"So, take the bay's reins and lead him!"

She nodded, seeing what the plan was. Rocky was to take the strain of the rope attached to Lucky. He was to walk away from the bank, accepting the weight, easing the palomino clear. But could he, *would* he do it?

She took the reins. "Walk on, Rocky!" she murmured.

Back in the muddy swamp, Lucky had stopped fighting.

He lay helpless, covered in mud and unrecognizable, waiting for rescue.

"Easy, boy!" Kirstie breathed instructions at the strong bay horse. "I know you warned us not to cross the creek, and you were right. So now it's up to you to save Lucky. Come on, Rocky, pull!"

The mustang understood exactly what was needed. He turned his back on the creek and took the strain. Every muscle in his body tensed, ready to heave. There was a dead weight behind, and silence from the spectators on the opposite bank. The only sound was of mud sucking and oozing around Lucky's exhausted body as Rocky pulled on the rope.

Seconds ticked by. The wet rope creaked. Nothing moved.

"It's no good! It's too tight around Lucky's neck!" Kirstie cried. She realized that the noose would cut into him and choke him.

"Wait!" It was Charlie's turn to come up with an idea. Running for a second rope, he unhitched one from Moose's saddle and brought it back to the creek. He aimed the noose at Lucky, swung it high above his head and threw. The loop hooked around the mud-caked saddle horn.

"Yes!" Kirstie hissed. She held out her hands to catch Charlie's end of the rope. "Now throw!"

The young wrangler sent the new rope whizzing across the creek. Kirstie caught with her good arm and wound it around Rocky's saddle. With two ropes secure, she ordered the bay horse forward once more.

By this time Lucky had regained the energy to help himself. He found firm rock beneath his back feet and pushed. His front legs thrashed through slime and mud, the ropes tightening as Rocky eased forward.

"Pull!" Kirstie whispered, her hand on the mustang's sweating neck.

He inched away from the bank, raising Lucky out of the swamp slowly, steadily.

"Some horse!" Charlie whistled his admiration as the strong stallion pulled.

"Don't let him give up!" Lisa urged.

Hadley stood silently watching the mustang tug the palomino to safety.

With a steadying hand on Rocky's shoulder, feeling his steely willpower concentrated on the act of rescue, Kirstie felt sure he would succeed. All she had to do was trust and wait.

The surface of the gray mud was smooth once more. There was nothing to signal the life and death struggle except trampled reeds by the bank of the creek.

On one side of Crystal Creek stood a small huddle of people: Lisa, Hadley and Charlie, with Sandy and Matt Scott. Sandy's red Dodge pickup was parked in the meadow. Moose, Crazy Horse and Cadillac grazed nearby.

"We came as soon as you radioed," Matt told Hadley.

The wrangler nodded. "Wasn't nothing you could do," he muttered. "But I knew you'd want to be here."

Sandy broke away and walked down to the bank. She stared anxiously across the water at the figures caked in mud; at Kirstie sitting on the ground, slumped forward and sobbing, at Rocky waiting by her side. "Hold on!" she called.

Kirstie raised her head and nodded. Mud covered every inch of her body. It had caked on her face, in her hair, plastering it to her skull. It was under her fingernails, inside every seam of her clothes. Wiping her hands on the grass, she dragged her hair back from her face and looked around for Lucky.

Her palomino stood next to the mustang. The ropes that had rescued him were still tied. He too was covered from head to foot in thick mud.

Kirstie's tears were tears of relief. Lucky was alive. Rocky had dragged him clear until his front feet found solid ground. The mustang hadn't let up for a second until the palomino was free of the swamp.

And they were proud tears. No other horse would have done for Lucky what Rocky had done. He was smarter, kinder, and more loyal than any horse she knew.

"We're crossing the creek higher upstream!" her mom called. "It's fine beyond the ridge. We'll be right with you!"

Kirstie stood up and went over to stand between Rocky and Lucky. "You knew that!" she said simply to the bay horse. The mustang's savvy must have shown him the safe crossing place. He'd even tried to warn her about the swamp.

When the others came to fetch them, carrying blankets to throw over the horses and wrap around Kirstie's shoulders, there were no harsh words, no blame for what Kirstie had done. There was more praise for Rocky from Charlie, who took off his saddle and rubbed him down. There were hugs for Lucky from a relieved Lisa, and kind words for Kirstie from her worried mom.

"But what about Rocky?" Kirstie begged. Her dream of freedom for him had sunk beneath the muddy swamp on the bank of Crystal Creek. The dreaded sale barn beckoned. "He saved Lucky's life. Doesn't that make up for him throwing me?"

Sandy shrugged and smiled. "That's not the way to look at it, honey, and you know it."

"What other way is there?"

"With some common sense and savvy," Matt put in, busy checking both horses for signs of injury.

"Horse savvy or human savvy?" Kirstie believed in a horse's instinct, but not what her brother called common sense. She believed that Rocky deserved better than the sale barn and turned to her mom, eyes fierce in his defense.

Sandy hesitated and turned to Hadley. "The big question is still the same; will Rocky ever be safe for guests to ride?"

Kirstie's gaze fixed on the head wrangler. He glanced at her. "No," he said.

She groaned and turned away.

". . . But," Hadley went on.

Kirstie swung around. She took a deep breath and listened.

121

"I always said Rocky's a fine horse. Not a guest horse, but a great mustang, all the same."

Matt finished his inspection of Lucky, untied the ropes that linked him to Rocky, and came around to listen. Sandy stood hands on hips, thinking carefully. Lisa was shoulder to shoulder with Kirstie, waiting for more.

"I ain't about to make a long speech," Hadley told them. "All I'm saying is, I can think of a way to use the horse so long as you can keep him out of reach of the roads."

"Which is?" Sandy said slowly.

"Use him as a staff horse at Half-Moon," the head wrangler explained. "He needs a good rider in the saddle, someone who knows horses, not a dude from the city."

"Meaning you, Hadley?" Matt thought he saw which way the old ranch hand's thoughts were heading.

"Nope." He shook his head and glanced around the listening group until his eyes lit on the person he was looking for. "I was thinking more about young Charlie here."

"Me?" Charlie let his mouth hang open. His tanned face reddened. "Are you serious?"

"Yes, of course!" Kirstie saw it in a flash. Charlie was the one who'd helped her with Rocky from the start; the only person who'd shared her faith in the problem horse. "Great!"

"Charlie?" Matt repeated, as if the thought had never crossed his mind.

"Hmm." Sandy let it sink in. "You mean, give Rocky to Charlie to head the trail rides?" She nodded slowly. "That would leave Moose free for a guest to ride. Yeah, that could work."

Lisa put her hands to her mouth. She turned away. Why wouldn't someone give the final word?

Kirstie held her breath. She saw Charlie's eyes light up. Hadley, who never praised anybody, who handed out the orders and went about his business, had just said that Charlie knew horses. That was worth more than a gold medal; more than anything to the junior wrangler. And, as if he had a sense of what was going on, Rocky had leaned forward to push his big, beautiful head over Charlie's shoulder.

"How long have you been thinking this way?" Sandy asked Hadley.

The old man shrugged. "A couple of weeks."

"But why didn't you say anything?" Lisa cried.

But Kirstie didn't care about any of that stuff. She stared at her mom, silently pleading for a decision.

Sandy Scott went up to the bay stallion and pushed his bedraggled, dark mane from his face. "You want to be Charlie's horse, eh, Rocky?"

The mustang blew gently on her hand. He blinked a couple of times, then nudged Charlie's shoulder.

". . . OK." Sandy smiled. "It's a deal."

Kirstie closed her eyes. Rocky could stay!

When she opened them again, Hadley was ready to get the horses back to the ranch. He gave Charlie orders to coil ropes and lift saddles. Matt was talking the solution through with Sandy, nodding and smiling. Then he went to help Charlie with his chores.

"Hey, Charlie, you gonna brush the mud off of this palomino when we get back?" Hadley called as he led Lucky upstream to cross the creek.

"Sure!" Charlie ran here and there, a wide grin on his face.

"Hey, Charlie, that bay of yours will need his jabs from the vet if he's gonna stay at the ranch. You gonna call Glen Woodford when we get back?"

"Yep!"

"And get him to check the palomino. And call the sale barn to say we're not bringing the bay in after all. And then there's bits needing cleaning, yards needing raking . . ."

"Yup, yup, yup!" Nothing could take the grin off Charlie's face.

Or wipe the feeling of incredible lightness out of Kirstie's heart. She stood by Crystal Creek looking up into Rocky's eyes. They were a clear, deep hazel, reflecting the light from the sky. They gazed steadily back at her, understanding everything.

Tomorrow she would wake up. Out of the window she would see Red Fox Meadow in the long, dew-laden shadow of Eagle's Peak. She would pick out Crazy Horse and Cadillac, Moose, Jitterbug and Silver Flash.

Lucky would be standing by the gate waiting for her as usual. At his side, most likely in a patch of early sunlight, she would see the bay coat and black mane of a beautiful stallion. He would glint copper in the rays of the sun. He would be looking up at the ranch house, maybe turn his head to the mountains for a second, then back to the house.

Then Charlie would walk out from the bunkhouse, hat low on his forehead, jacket collar turned up. He would stride to the meadow to fetch his horse. Rocky would see him and trot along the fence to greet him. Charlie would slip on a headcollar, open the gate, and lead him out. Horse and man, heading to the corral to start a day's work.

"That's how it's gonna be!" she whispered to Rocky.

The horse nodded in the direction of Lucky and the others heading back to Half-Moon Ranch. He nudged her with his nose: *Come on, Let's go*!